Table of Contents

4   The Monster at the End of the World
Story by Lee Clark Zumpe
Illustration by Laura Givens

13   Black Holiness
Poem by Raymond H.V. Gallucci

14   Steampunk's Tell-Tale Beginning
Story by Charles Chapman & David Van Houten
Illustration by Jag Lall

17   The Warm Machine
Poem by Alexandra de Romen

18   High Maintenance
Story by Vaughn Wright
Illustration by Laura Givens

23   Lamia
Poem by Karin L. Frank

24   Black Orchid
Story by Rick Novy
Illustration by Jag Lall

30   The Darkest Part of the Forest
Story by C.J. Killmer
Illustration by Neil T. Foster

34   Lemon Wind
Poem by Lyn Lifshin

35   Early to Bed.....Late to Rise
Poem by Gary W. Davis

36   Whose Life is it Anyway?
Cartoon by Jerry Shippee

40   Ragtime: What Rough Beast
Story by T. Fox Dunham
Illustration by Paul Niemiec

46   The Machine Planet
Poem by K.S. Hardy

48   Geroge Lucas's Lost Flying Saucer
Story by Richard P. Nixon
Illustration by Kathy Ferrell

54   First Contact
Flash Fiction by M.E. Brines

55   Speaking Cicada
Poem by Gary Every

56   Demons of Disease
Story by Abra Staffin-Wiebe
Illustration by Laura Givens

59   Post Funeral Mission (to Mars)
Poem by Jason Sturner

60   Competition
Story by Mike Wilson
Illustration by Paul Niemiec

69   Globes
Poem by G.O. Clark

70   I Will Upload to the Metabase No More Forever
Story by Dan Manning
Illustration by Laura Givens

77   The Bridge is Out
Poem by Neal Wilgus

78   Searching for King Arthur's Grave
Story by Gary Every
Illustration by Kathy Ferrell

81   The Skip Tracer
Poem by L.B. Sedlacek

81   Behind the Walls
Poem by R. Donald James Gauveau

82   Warden of the Dry Plain
Story by Aaron Polson
Illustration by Laura Givens

86   The Goat
Story by K.S. Hardy
Illustration by Laura Givens

90   An Elephant in the Living Room
Story by Christine Marie Angela
Illustration by Laura Givens

92   Strawberry Milkshake
Poem by Lauren McBride

94   To See If It Is Possible
Story by Erin K. Wagner
Illustration by Morland Gonsoulin

100   Kings of Glass
Poem by Linda Neuer

102   Talisman Book Reviews
Reviews by Robert E. Porter, David Lee Summers, and Neal Wilgus

105   About the Contributors

> **Front Cover by Laura Givens**

Mad Science

In my years as an astronomer, I've participated in some pretty crazy experiments. As an undergraduate, I worked with a friend to build a six-foot tall Tesla coil. Although we shorted components out in spectacular ways, it prompted my undergraduate advisor to say that I would either wind up as a top notch empiricist or a serial killer. It also brought my electronic skills to notice, which helped me land a job with Dr. Stirling Colgate in graduate school.

Back in 1964, Colgate had the crazy idea of using a computer to control a telescope to search for supernovae. One colleague even mocked him, saying the only reason he was doing the work was so he could do astronomy from the bar. In the 80's, I worked with Colgate to help him upgrade his telescope and include more objects in the search. Unfortunately, the telescope never discovered any supernovae, novae, or other interesting objects, but it did prove one could use a computer to control a telescope. At the turn of the century, I once saw a list that showed the 100 greatest contributions to astronomy in the 20th century. Albert Einstein was on the list once. Stephen Hawking was on the list once. Only one person made the list twice—Stirling Colgate, for predicting that supernova explosions would be preceded by a neutrino burst, and for inventing automated astronomy.

In the 1990s, while working at Kitt Peak, Dr. Saul Perlmutter called up periodically asking for observations of supernovae. This interrupted observations and tended to annoy people who were scheduled. Why couldn't he get devoted time on a smaller telescope? Again, more mad science. As it turns out, his observations showed the universe was accelerating. In 2011, Saul Perlmutter won the Nobel Prize for his contributions toward the discovery of Dark Energy.

This issue of *Tales of the Talisman* contains several stories of mad science. Elder gods use the Large Hadron Collider to break through to our world. In the nineteenth century, doctors developing an artificial heart drive a neighbor to madness. Thomas Edison attempts to contact the dead. Kids find a suspiciously realistic flying saucer left behind by George Lucas. Sometimes mad science leads to great things. Other times it leads to disaster. Turn the page and see where these tales of mad science lead you.

— David Lee Summers

Tales of the
Talisman

Volume 10   Issue 2

ISBN: 1-885093-76-4

William Grother
Publisher

David Lee Summers
Editor

Laura Givens
Art Director

Kumie Wise
Assistant Editor

Tales of the Talisman
(ISSN 1558-0377)
is published quarterly by
Hadrosaur Productions
P.O. Box 2194
Mesilla Park, NM 88047-2194
www.hadrosaur.com

Subscriptions: $24.00 per year
$48.00 per two years
Subscriptions available at:
www.talesofthetalisman.com

The Monster at the End of the World

Story by Lee Clark Zumpe   Illustration by Laura Givens

1.

Initially, they blamed the incident on terrorists.

Centered on the Franco-Swiss border near Geneva, the blast took out a significant amount of countryside, destroying the world's largest and highest-energy particle accelerator and sending up a plume of debris that eventually circled the Northern Hemisphere and played havoc with air traffic. The event registered as an 8.2 on the Richter scale. Thousands perished in the initial explosion, with total deaths estimated at more than 118,500 after two weeks.

The Americans leapt at the opportunity to rattle their swords, while the European Union took a more cautious approach, pouring billions of euros into the ensuing investigation. Because of toxicity levels, ground zero had to be cordoned off and nearby municipalities evacuated. Citizens had to be relocated. The United Nations provided 2,000 ground troops—fresh from active duty in Afghanistan and Sudan—to secure the perimeter. That number would increase fourfold in the coming months, significantly supplemented by U.S. Special Operations Forces, led jointly by officers of the Strategic Support Branch, Task Force 13 and the Office of Strategic Preservation.

The undertaking, dubbed OPERATION BOTTLECAP by the Pentagon, effectively extinguished all the live footage that had been flowing freely from the area for weeks—including video of some inexplicable phenomena that created an overnight sensation on the Internet. Meanwhile, world governments spoon-fed the gullible media tangential stories designed to distract the horrified masses.

In other words, everyone pretty much played by the book.

Six months after the conflagration that might have ended the world, the EU committee investigating the incident released its findings and issued a statement concluding that "due to a lack of evidence, the precise cause of the LHC disaster cannot be pinpointed. While sabotage cannot be ruled out," the report stated—at the insistence of the military-industrial complex, "there simply isn't enough information upon which to base any claims of culpability."

Case closed, for all intents and purposes.

That's about the time my phone rang. My name is Clayton Kopec, slayer of wannabe gods, crusty demonic minions and a wide variety of malevolent creatures. I'm a regional director for the secret federal agency known as the Office of Strategic Preservation. Sure, it sounds like one of the countless agencies gobbled up by the Department of Homeland Security, but it actually operates under the radar. Way under the radar.

As an example of just how cloak-and-dagger this clandestine organization can be, I would cite the top secret case file pertaining to the Murg Valley expedition and the re-emergence of Walther Wulff and other Ahnenerbe diehards in 1974, an event which culminated in the detonation of a small-yield nuclear device in central Europe. Does anyone remember seeing pictures of the mushroom cloud rising against the backdrop of the Bavarian Alps? Does anyone remember hearing Walter Cronkite mention the incident on the evening news?

Didn't think so.

"Kopec." I glanced at the clock on the night-stand, partially obscured by a bottle of sparkling water that had lost its fizz hours earlier. From what I could see, the sun would not rise for another three hours.

"You're going to visit your aunt in Geneva." I recognized the gravelly voice as belonging to Walter Lawrence, my mentor and the current director of the OSP. "She's taken ill—some kind of viral infection, from what I understand." He paused, allowing me a moment to consider the news. "She doesn't have long, I'm afraid. You may need to arrange for services while there."

The one-way conversation ended abruptly with a muffled click.

Of course, I had no aunt in Geneva. According to Lawrence's instructions, the situation in Europe had deteriorated. The "viral infection" indicated a significant incursion of extra-dimensional invasive entities (a bacterial infection would have represented extraterrestrial entities). While the situation was serious, the infiltration was being inhibited for the moment; had my "aunt" been "on death's door," the implication would have been that within 48 hours, all hell would break loose.

Still, I did not waste any time chartering a private flight to Switzerland through the traditional contractor. If the world was about to end, I wanted front row seats.

That bit about needing "to arrange for services"—that's Lawrence's euphemism for calling in a nuclear strike.

2.

Cruising some 50,000 feet above the Atlantic in a Gulfstream G550, I found my gaze drawn to the pale cerulean band along the horizon, gently tracing the curve of the Earth.

Below, the cloud deck stretched endlessly, blanketing the ocean. Above, the stratosphere darkened dramatically, as if bowing beneath the weight of the cosmos. Nowhere is the irrelevancy of human civilization—let alone the individual—more evident than from a great distance above the hopelessly insignificant celestial body my species named Earth. I had seen the planet once from the thermosphere, and the impression is even more overwhelming at greater altitudes.

That life had developed here was improbable; that the planet had managed to sustain higher forms of life for any length of time seemed inconceivable. Yet, humanity, threatened ceaselessly by total annihilation, had somehow managed to survive … thus far. As if the catalog of common extinction level events weren't enough to impede our progress, in addition to species-decimating hazards such as impact events, supervolcanoes, pandemics and gamma ray bursts, the inhabitants of Earth also had endured the acrimony of somnolent alien entities, transdimensional nomads and obscure rival lifeforms.

A buzz on my laptop alerted me to an incoming call.

"Sorry to have to pull you out of your semi-retirement, old boy," Lawrence said, though a certain buoyancy in his tone diminished any hint of sincerity. Moving from a field agent position to a "cushy desk job" as regional director qualified as retirement in his eyes. "What we're looking at here is a geostationary temporal rift, affixed in spacetime by some unrecognizable technology," Lawrence said.

I had been expecting an e-briefing for more than an hour. The low-resolution video image made him look 20 years older. Before he could continue, I popped in earphones so as not to bother the other passengers.

There were no other passengers.

"'Unrecognizable' or not at liberty to divulge?"

"TBOC," Lawrence said—Totally Beyond Our Comprehension.

In other words, the well-meaning particle physicists at CERN inadvertently punched a hole in the fibrous membrane of spacetime and something on the other end managed to wedge its foot—or tentacle—in the rift before it could reseal itself.

"Even if the LHC caused a breach in spacetime, it should've evaporated in a microsecond," I said, thinking out loud. According to my limited understanding of infinitesimal calculus and mathematical physics, Cauchy radiation theoretically acted to seal any such rifts. "If it's being sustained artificially," I said, though I doubted the SOP had misjudged the situation, "whatever intelligence acted upon it must have moved incredibly fast."

"I know what you're getting at," Lawrence said. "I think whatever we're dealing with had foreknowledge, too."

"Can't we seal it from our end?"

"Yes," he said, but I could hear the hesitation in his voice. "That's only part of the problem, though." The agency's lab coat coalition had developed some ingenious containment mechanisms over the years, shielding Earth from all kinds of apocalyptic horrors and unfriendly entities of the Must-Not-Be-Named strain. "We appear to be dealing with a catabolic force majeure … or a retrochronological lifeform."

"That's … new." I had read plenty of dry textbook copy concerning the characteristics of temporal anomalies in the agency's mandated continuing education series. Even with all of my experience in dealing with meta-dimensional fissures, artificial wormholes and interdimensional conduits, I could never fully grasp the intricacies of the subject. "How did you arrive at that conclusion?"

"Our first reconnaissance drone estimated the terminus to be approximately 1,140 years from the date of the incident," he said nonchalantly, as though sending a remotely operated vehicle hundreds of years into the future—and maintaining communications with it—had become old hat for him. "A second ROV, an armed robotic armored vehicle, revised the date, bringing it down to 1,070 years."

"That's only a 200-year discrepancy," I said. "Well within the margin of error."

"Obviously," Lawrence said. "But each subsequent reading has moved the date backwards. Once we realized it wasn't an instrumentation error, we began monitoring the rate of regression at regular intervals." Lawrence paused, shifting his gaze to another monitor to check the most recent data. "The terminus is moving back at a rate of approximately 70 years for every week we move forward."

"What aren't you telling me?" I knew Lawrence well enough to recognize that he was holding the good news for the punch line.

"Well," he said, trying carefully to choose the

optimum words to underscore the situation. "From the visuals we've received, things are looking pretty grim at the terminus. Grim enough to displace a few marginal players, steering them right back through the hole." That explained the grainy viral videos of gelatinous shoggoths making the rounds on You-Tube—gummy rats leaving a sinking ship. "We're seeing total desolation outside the temporal bubble. Imagine an unavoidable casualty with enough energy to propel itself backwards through time, destroying everything on the planet over and over again."

"How long do we have?"

"Right now, best estimates put the end of the world about 30 years from now," he said casually. "By the time you're standing on ground zero, we'll be down to 20 years."

3.

A brisk walk across the newly refurbished tarmac in Geneva delivered me to a waiting Hummer Limo and a skittish young agency gopher with a wiry frame and a frail handshake. The airport—which had been all but flattened the day the LHC was destroyed—had been rebuilt to utilitarian standards: Travel to and from the region was strictly controlled. The facility had become, nonetheless, a hub of chaos.

On the approach, the Gulfstream G550 had flown over both ground zero and the city of Geneva. The scarred landscape that formerly housed CERN provided a sobering hint at the power unleashed six months earlier, virtually disintegrating a chunk of the Swiss plateau and leaving a chasm nearly 10 miles wide and 750 feet deep. Around the perimeter of the vast gorge, a barricade had been erected, punctuated by dozens of watchtowers. A virtual city of tents stood nearby, providing temporary shelter for those patrolling the area.

The center of the abyss had been covered by what appeared to be the beginnings of an enormous geodesic dome that, when complete, would enshroud the entire disaster zone.

Dozens of buildings in neighboring Geneva had collapsed. The ensuing fallout had buried whole city blocks and left islands of debris in Lake Geneva. Most inhabitants had been forcibly removed, scattered through a network of refugee camps across Europe.

Yet, all of this paled in comparison to the coming catastrophe.

"Mr. Kopec, I presume," the gawky kid said, opening the car door for me.

"That's right, Slim." I handed him the duffle bag into which I had unceremoniously crammed a few days' worth of clothes, toiletries and two bestsellers I had been intending to read, in the unlikely event that beer-thirty came early and without further casualties. "Take me to the suck."

Inside the white Hummer Limousine, I found a makeshift war room with a flat-screen digital map detailing the landscape around ground zero, six work-stations with top-of-the-line computer set-ups, a small armory, three cutting-edge high-hazard pressure suits and a very interesting 3-D display that appeared to chart temporal anomalies in the vicinity in real-time.

Before I could ask Slim—who hadn't offered a name—why I needed three pressure suits, I noticed that I was sharing the E-ticket ride into tomorrow.

"Clayton, good to see you." I recognized Ian Barlow's voice before my eyes had adjusted to the dim lighting. "I knew the Yanks would send in the cavalry."

Seeing Barlow, the British point-man for potentially hostile confrontations with non-human combatants, offered a glimmer of hope in an otherwise hopeless situation. I had worked with Barlow on a number of occasions and knew he could A) Think on his feet, B) Crack the toughest exoskeleton and drain the acidic pus out of the nastiest beastie's venom sac, and C) Exterminate a horde of belligerent agents (human or otherwise) without losing his focus or his unique sense of humor.

"They volunteered you for this kamikaze run, too?"

"Wouldn't want to miss the apocalypse," he said. Well into his 50s—a good five years older than me—Barlow kept fit and agile. "Someone will have to throw a spanner into the works."

The third suit belonged to none other than Eliza Hayes, theoretical physicist and radical chaos occultist. Her treatises on quantum metaphysics, time dilation and spacetime topology had forced the OSP to rewrite its operational handbook.

"Hey Clayton," she said, avoiding eye contact. Former lovers have a tendency to do that, particularly when the relationship ends on a sour note. "How have you been?"

"Well," I started, flipping through a dozen cynical responses. Fortunately, I bit my tongue and opted for a civil reply: "I'm good," I said, sounding more than a little bit like a scolded child. "You?"

"Feeling a bit pessimistic at the moment." We

had parted ways more than three years ago after a decade-long affair. We shared everything, from closet space to ammunition. "The PTB picked a scientist, a diplomat and a soldier as their all-star lineup, and I'm not sure we'll even be able to agree on a game plan."

"'Diplomat?'" I didn't care for the analogy. Furthermore, if the PTB—Powers That Be—considered this permutation to be the most viable option, I wasn't going to argue with them. "I prefer to think of myself as the Wild West Lawman, a combination of Wyatt Earp and James T. Kirk. Diplomacy, yes; but only when supported by firepower."

The Hummer Limo jerked forward and sped toward a gate on the opposite side of the runway. I settled into a seat in front of a work station.

"Firepower shouldn't be a problem," Hayes said, shooting a withering glare in Barlow's general direction. "G.I. Joe here has a new toy and he's itching for fireworks."

"Not so much," Barlow said. "If I poke the Big Red Button, we'll all be dancing in the fires of fission."

"Which will accomplish nothing," Hayes said. "You aren't seeing the big picture. This whole thing is a conundrum." She seemed tired, frustrated. I could tell she had thought this thing through backwards and forwards a thousand times. For her, hell was the unsolvable puzzle. Internally, she would rearrange the pieces continuously until obsession eclipsed her sanity. "The world ended six months ago. We aren't survivors—we're just oblivious to the fact that we're already dead."

While I realized she was speaking metaphorically, I wondered if she might be a liability.

"Okay, you need a new pair of eyes on the equation," I said, trying to change the course of her negativity. "Scenario one: We jump through the hole into the future, look around, find the off switch and doomsday stops hurling backwards through time. Mission accomplished."

"Except that means the world will end in 20 years," Barlow pointed out. Good point.

"Scenario two," I continued, trying to sound confident. "We jump through the hole into the future, look around, find whatever entity is responsible for this and make him put things right."

"Are you that persuasive," Hayes asked. The skepticism in her eyes told me she already knew the answer. "You'll have approximately 40 minutes to reason with it before the temporal bubble collapses and we more than likely become the last three fatalities

of the planet."

"Any entity that has enough power at its disposal to screw with physics like this is unlikely to participate in direct negotiations," I said, paraphrasing a tenet from the agency's handbook. "Mediation through third-party entities might prove advantageous, but…"

"But 40 minutes doesn't give you much time to have tea and crumpets with the Monster at the End of the World," Barlow said. "Which moves us to scenario three: We blow it to Kingdom Come."

"Which, again, means the world ends in 20 years," I said, offering a nod to Hayes for that unsettling epiphany. "Of course, sacrificing our future would mean saving our past, I suppose. But that doesn't sit too well with me."

"Pretty much any way you look at it," Barlow said, "we're flies waiting for the windshield on the highway."

4.

An hour later, we found ourselves standing on a platform about 60 feet above the bottom of the gorge. A flight of stairs led to a murky pond hovering in thin air, its surface roughly perpendicular to the ground. A metal gangplank extended forward into the gap in spacetime, disappearing beneath its undulating face.

The floor of the recently-formed canyon looked like a small industrial park, complete with warehouses, elevated prefabricated riveted-steel water tanks, diesel tanks, office facilities, utilities, two traveling-cranes and a dozen Quonset huts. Encircling the focal point of the temporal anomaly, OSP's lab coat coalition had designed a large-scale Coulomb Bulwark, effectively stabilizing the aperture. A connecting ramp led to a modified freight elevator which was clearly being used to transport any entities that managed to use the rupture as an escape hatch to avoid doomsday. I'm sure all the usual suspects had shambled through the portal—Shoggoths, Chthonian larvae and the abominable Tcho-Tchos all possessed an ability to sense disruptions in spacetime and would be drawn to the rift like zombies to an old-folks home.

A fire-fighting hose rested on a nearby reel affixed to the makeshift control room that had been built to monitor the temporal anomaly. Temperatures in the vicinity fluctuated dramatically, I presumed—rips in spacetime tend to generate a great deal of background radiation. Small conflagrations might erupt at any moment.

The hose could also be used to pressure wash the platform. Shoggoths were a messy lot.

"Team Alpha," the voice sounded crystal clear, though static both preceded and followed it. We had all suited up after our arrival—an awkward demonstration involving three would-be heroes mucking about in their skivvies while trying to listen to a bullet-list training drill led by Slim without the benefit of a Microsoft PowerPoint presentation. "Prepare to transit the temporal aperture."

Compared to my two colleagues, I felt a bit naked. Hayes toted a sleek multi-wheel titanium travel case, no doubt filled with an assortment of gauges and scientific paraphernalia that would allow her to probe and prod whatever waited for us at the terminus. Barlow carried his nuclear firecracker in a ripstop wool backpack and could trigger it from a control pad on his wrist. He also sported a number of Very Big Guns capable of inflicting catastrophic damage.

I had my trusty laptop with translation software, a modified amplifier and a set of small but high-tech speakers. The whole compact package would enable me to whisper an appropriate string of verbal commands—known in occult circles as a binding spell—to sway the architect of this doomsday scenario back into dormancy … maybe. It's like pillow talk, directed at one of the Great Old Ones.

I know … sounds a lot like diplomacy.

Unlike most diplomats, though, I had a number of choice weapons at my disposal—many of them utterly intangible. Likely to be of most value under the circumstances was my hyper-intuition, a kind of acute perceptivity that affords what laymen call a "sixth sense." Let's put it this way: Put me in a pitch-black room with a hostile party and I'll put a bullet between his eyes in under a second, regardless of how much noise he may be making.

In identifying and evaluating the entity responsible for all of this, I knew I could count on the call-a-friend network I had established during the course of my career. Not all non-humans were hostile, after all—and many could be persuaded to become allies in certain situations. At the very least, they could be strong-armed into revealing chinks in armor, faults and failings or other vulnerabilities that could be exploited.

I also had four decades of experience with non-Eucledean calculus and fourth-order variegated differential equations so complex they could give Cthulhu a migraine. Who says higher mathematics isn't useful in the real world?

The ride from the airport took far less time than we needed to come up with a strategy. The discussion never matured into anything more than hawkish threats (Barlow), bitter lamentations (Hayes) and a unanimous expression of stupefaction.

"Good luck and Godspeed," the voice from Mission Control said, and I sensed Barlow—on my right, impatiently stepping forward into the spacetime puncture. "See you back in 40 minutes."

We took four steps. I winced as the anomaly first touched my face mask. An instant later, we stood at Ground Zero, some 20 years in the future.

It had been a sweltering afternoon a moment earlier. An LCD display on the inner surface of my face mask indicated the temperature had dropped roughly 80 degrees. The cutting-edge high-hazard pressure suit came equipped with a climate control which immediately compensated, though I felt a brief rush of surprising iciness.

The sun had abandoned the sky—or rather, the sun and sky had changed. The scope of impact was far wider than anticipated: In this not-so-distant future, the world withered beneath a cooling sun which itself faced a premature death. Just above the rim of the canyon, the cracked and shadowy face of a battered moon lingered, adrift in a peculiarly low orbit and surrounded by a greenish cloud of dust and rock.

Beneath our feet, the platform remained—though the dilapidated scaffold upon which it rested swayed worryingly.

The warehouses and water and diesel tanks all lay in various states of ruin. Office facilities, windowless and charred, showed no sign of recent occupation. The Quonset huts had been shredded and displaced. The cranes had toppled. The freight elevator survived, though it sagged to one side and threatened to collapse at any moment.

I looked first to Hayes and found her squatting over her travel-case, taking various measurements and interpreting the data. Barlow, on the other hand, was surveying the situation, mulling the ramifications and assessing the situation.

"Not safe here," I said, and immediately found agreement in his eyes. My on-the-spot deduction had as much to do with the aging, rickety framework as it did with the possibility of some unfriendly lurkers in the shadows—although I was starting to get the impression we weren't alone. "Need to move. Get down to ground level."

"No," Hayes said, even as I grasped her shoulder to urge her to relocate. She had hunkered down on the platform and was preparing to activate a number of small drones she had personally designed. These would scatter around the immediate area and provide real-time data on any other temporal anomalies. "We should stay in the proximity of the…"

My heart skipped a bit when she failed to finish the sentence. Instinctively, I knew what she had realized.

I turned around slowly. Where there should have been a good-sized rip in spacetime, there was nothing.

"Oh, that really sucks."

"No, wait," Hayes said. "It's still here. It's just shifted a little."

Of course it had. At least two of the six pylons that made up the Coulomb Bulwark had completely disintegrated. While it may have been a geostationary temporal rift, it could still be repositioned by external forces like earthquakes, nuclear war and planetary impacts. From the looks of things, Earth had seen one or more of those events in the recent past.

"Can you locate it?" Barlow tapped me on the arm and pointed toward the upper ledge of the gorge. Something was up there. "Can you find the aperture?"

"I can't," Hayes said. At that moment, a dozen small heli-drones lifted off from the platform, scattering in all directions. "But they can."

5.

Wandering around a post-apocalyptic world isn't half as much fun as Hollywood would have us believe. Over the next few minutes, we found no intelligent speaking apes, no crazy Australians in armored cars searching for water and gasoline, no oversized scorpions and man-eating cockroaches, no sentient plants, no zombies, no vampires and no armies of narcissistic robots.

Much to my chagrin, we also found no Great Old Ones—ultra-powerful alien beings whose understanding of highly advanced technologies often lead lesser beings to mistake them for gods. Frankly, I had expected to find a number of these near-omnipotent beings stretched out like snowbirds on a Florida beach in wintertime, kicking up their heels (or hooves or feelers) and patting each other on the back for finally eradicating the pesky human race.

Mind you, with my visibility limited to a small crater in central Europe, I didn't *know* that they weren't to blame—but I *felt* it, thanks to my hyper-intuition. And I could confirm that scenario very easily.

"Any luck yet?" We had managed to reach ground level and had set up a provisional base camp, hoping we would not need it for more than a few minutes. "Have you ever tested these drones before?"

"Not exactly," Hayes admitted. "I know they're functional, but as far as actually having an opportunity to field test them … well, it's not like temporal anomalies pop up in my apartment on a regular basis."

"No," I said, "Just culinary anomalies." Hayes could disassemble and reassemble any technological gizmo set in front of her. Somehow, that wisdom did not extend to cooking equipment such as microwave ovens, stoves, toasters and coffee makers. I saw the hint of smile on her face before she replaced it with a grimace. "Sorry, couldn't help myself."

"I could use one of your world-famous Italian dishes right about now," Hayes admitted. "I'm famished."

"Enough banter, you two," Barlow said. "Find our way home first, then you can enjoy a touching reunion."

"And we still have to, you know, stop the end of the world," I reminded him. "Except,"

"Except what?"

"Except, I don't think there's anyone on this end to deal with." I knelt, digging in an exterior pocket for a piece of chalk—never leave home without one. On the ground, I started tracing out a particularly nasty bit of high calculus, the kind of thing you see scratched on dry-erase boards in shadowy Miskatonic classrooms presided over by gibbering mathematicians. Peculiar as it may seem, complicated equations tend to attract the attention of some of the more highly evolved entities lurking about the multiverse. "Let's see if I can get something to corroborate."

A moment later, a short, white-haired, bipedal being coalesced from the chalk dust. He looked like a cross between Yoda and a tree sloth. With his saucer-shaped eyes he examined his surroundings.

He was frightened.

"Guys, meet Surgat," I said. "Sometimes, he's mistaken for the Jersey Devil."

Barlow and Hayes seemed unimpressed.

"Can I go now," Surgat asked, his voice no more than a buzz between my ears. "I should not have come back."

"Just one question," I said. Surgat, who had a reputation as someone who could open all locks, kept tabs on both dimensional and temporal portals throughout the universe. He knew who used them and he knew who created them. "Who caused this?"

"No one here," he said quietly. "No one left at all, all gone—except, the Brân Lwyd, the carrion-feeders who plague dying worlds."

"Who then? What's sustaining this anomaly?"

"He who dwells in the center of your world, accompanied by his infernal pipers," Surgat said with a shudder. "The all-seeing eye corrupted one of your kind, who acted as his agent begetting this awful calamity. It shall take all those he serves, eventually, stretching across space and time back to the birth of this universe. Unchallenged, he will reshape all things, letting chaos reign."

While I doubted the scale of Surgat's assessment, Nyarlathotep could continue to tug the anomaly back through time, preventing life from ever taking root upon the Earth. I could confront The Crawling Chaos if necessary, possibly call upon other forces capable of stopping this madness. There was only one problem.

Nyarlathotep did not exist here anymore. He likely took refuge in the distant past.

An instant later, Surgat vanished, leaving me with no way to resolve the crisis.

"I've found it," Hayes said. "I've found several, actually."

"What do you mean," Barlow said.

"I've found the original rift," she said. "It will take us 10 minutes to reach it." Considering the fact that we had already spent nearly 30 minutes at the end of the world, a 10-minute march seemed reasonable. "The probes have found dozens of smaller portals, leading to different time periods."

"How do you know that," I asked. I knew that she could locate temporal anomalies; I didn't know she could determine what waited on the opposite side. "Just what kind of technology are you using?"

"The heli-drones are equipped with a super-bradyon transmitter," she explained. "I theorized that they could be used to transmit data through a rift. Apparently, it worked."

"So we could theoretically go back in time and prevent the entire event," Barlow said. "Bloody brilliant."

"Not so fast," Hayes said. "As far as I can tell, all of the termini are temporally located from the moment of the disaster at the LHC to about seven or eight months later."

"That would figure," I said. "So the best we can hope for is going back to that moment in hopes of shutting down the LHC before it goes boom."

"Or," Barlow said, "making a different kind of boom."

"Are you suggesting what I think you're suggesting?" I had known Barlow for 20 years, had worked with him on a number of predicaments that had the potential to take down civilization as we know it. I knew he would do what was necessary to save humanity. Still, he had never been the type to sacrifice lives for the greater good. Somehow, we'd always managed to find a way to avoid casualties altogether. "That's not an option we've considered."

"It seems to be our only option," Barlow said. "Look—this little nuke will take out the facility, but it won't inflict the level of damage the original blast did. We're talking a couple thousand at ground zero vs. nearly 120,000 deaths plus the eventual end of the world."

"What if it doesn't work," I said. "What if the chain reaction is already in progress, and you're just lighting a match on the face of the sun?"

"Well, then we tried," Barlow said. "You two go back and work on Plan B."

"There's no Plan B," Hayes said. "I don't see any alternatives, in fact."

"Tell me where I need to go," Barlow said.

"We're all heading in the same direction," Hayes said, abandoning her travel case. She carried only one small handheld. "I'll get you there in three minutes."

"Come on, Kopec," Barlow said. "Time for me to go save the world."

So much for diplomacy. I suddenly felt obsolete.

6.

The carrion-feeders—the Brân Lwyd, as Surgat called them—began oozing down the sides of the canyon while we headed towards the temporal rift. Rather like jellyfish with spider legs, the things posed no immediate threat. Had they wanted to attack, sheer numbers would have given them the upper hand in a confrontation.

Nevertheless, when one strayed too close to the team, we took the necessary steps.

Barlow tossed me one of his Very Big Guns so that I could provide some form of usefulness. I took a few potshots, missing the first two and nailing the third and fourth.

I had no experience with the Brân Lwyd, but I could easily work out their nature. Like all carrion-feeders, they appeared almost magically at the appropriate moment—long enough after death so as not to find themselves endangered, but soon enough after that the dead had not completely putrefied. Of course, these creatures seemed less interested in rotting corpses—and there were quite a few of those lying around, by the way—than they were in the relics of civilization itself.

They appeared particularly fascinated, for instance, in the Quonset huts, which they engulfed and devoured greedily.

It was about that time that I had an unsettling sense of déjà vu. Seeing the slimy blobs leaching onto bits of machinery and gliding over wreckage stirred up images in my mind of a similar scene and engendered thoughts I knew I had reflected upon at some other time.

I fell behind as I contemplated the situation, scanning the landscape more critically. I recognized far too many elements for this to be a coincidence.

"Keep moving," Barlow said, a trace of annoyance emerging in his voice. "No time to waste, Kopec."

"How much farther," I asked, picking up the pace.

Hayes would say *200 feet*, I thought.

"200 feet," Hayes said. "That will put Barlow right in front of his portal. The one we're looking for is another 1,200 feet to the east."

A moment later we came to a standstill. Before us, a small temporal aperture swirled and pulsated rhythmically. Unlike the one we had previously transited, this one was alluringly translucent, offering distorted images of what lay at the terminus. It appeared to open in the midst of a long corridor deep inside the LHC. In the distance, a number of researchers could be seen inspecting equipment.

"Home," Hayes said. "Certainly looks a lot more inviting than this place."

"Same place," Barlow reminded her. "What a difference a few decades can make, huh?"

My gaze, however, had shifted by that time.

I was looking at the muddy ground. There, I found far more footprints than there should have been. Each footprint, however, matched the tracks we made with our boots.

Anxiously, I looked over my shoulder.

I saw three individuals standing atop the platform.

How many times had we already done this?

"Hayes," I said. "If he goes back in time, won't there be two of him co-existing in the same period? Isn't that some kind of a temporal no-no."

"Well, yes, technically," she said. "But he won't be there for very long, Clay. There's no chance of them meeting. Besides, once the temporal bubble collapses, he would effectively cease to exist."

"So, once he's through, he's got a couple of minutes to detonate?"

"Precisely two minutes and 25 seconds," she said, glancing at her clock. "And that's exactly what we have if we want to get home."

That was all the information I needed. I grabbed Hayes by the arm, raised my Very Big Gun and blasted Barlow. I jumped through the vortex, dragging Hayes behind me.

On the other side, it took about five seconds to blow the face mask and dig a cell phone out of an external pocket. While Hayes pounded on my pressure suit, I left myself a very concise message on my home voice mail:

"Ian Barlow compromised, possible agent of Nyarlathotep. LHC disaster averted, temporal anomaly contained. Future safeguards required, suggest building a Coulomb Bulwark around the collider. Invite Eliza Hayes over for lasagna. Contact Surgot for further…"

7.

At first, I thought the message was a prank.

Fortunately, Surgot's memory doesn't get garbled by these kinds of phenomena and he filled in all the empty spaces for me.

For someone who had no recollection of the entire event, Walter Lawrence was quite grateful for my services and offered me another promotion, which I declined. I did insist that he involve Eliza Hayes in retrofitting the LHC to avoid any future mishaps.

Having never had the opportunity to detonate the small warhead that would have set off the temporal chain reaction, Ian Barlow was nonetheless arrested and imprisoned.

I would like to think that This Island Earth had survived the incident unscathed, since, in fact, the incident did not actually happen. The problem is—it did happen. Only by a stroke of luck and innate instinct did civilization get to rewrite the outcome of this particular calamity, though the ripples it generated will be broadcast throughout the multiverse. Those near-omnipotent things that inhabit the farthest corners of space and time will chortle over the incident.

Likewise, those with vested interests will see how corruptible our most staunch defenders may be and how ultimately fragile our defenses have become.

Black Holiness

"Into the singularity's"
A fantasy or parody
That offers much hilarity
Because it can't exist.

Once Maxwell brought some clarity
To laws derived by Faraday,
No more was there disparity
In mind of physicist.

For Einstein gave the guarantee
That black hole's not a rarity,
Though Schwarzschild showed emphatically
They're willows-of-the-wisp.

Once Hilbert erred mathematically.
There came full circularity
That such were the reality
That none could dare resist.

So if you seek camaraderie
And physics popularity,
Don't utter such vulgarity
As "Black holes are a myth."

— Raymond H.V. Gallucci

Author's note: Based on "The Black Hole, the Big Bang, and Modern Physics" webpage by Stephen J. Crothers. http://www.sjcrothers.plasmaresources.com

Steampunk's Tell-Tale Beginning

Story by Charles Chapman
& David Van Houten

Illustration by Jag Lall

In a small apartment converted into a makeshift science laboratory, two men put the final changes on the monstrosity that filled half the room with brass fittings, pipes seemingly haphazardly connected, and various valves and knobs spread out at assorted junctures. In the middle of everything were two metal water tanks; the larger of the two was an elevated reservoir for the smaller, both of which were built on top of two reinforced coal stoves, which were burning.

As they stepped back to admire their creation, the older man, Dr. Llewellyn, shook his head. "I can't believe we are finally finished."

The younger man, Dr. Smythe, grinned at his colleague. "Six months of hard work, but it will be worth it—if it works."

"It will work. We've tested every scenario—the science is solid," said Dr. Llewellyn, raising his bushy, graying eyebrows.

"Shall we test it then?"

Llewellyn looked out the window at the dark violet, Victorian London skyline. "It must be after one by now."

"And?" Smythe interjected impatiently. "Aren't you curious if we were successful?"

"Yes … yes, get the circulatory system, and I'll get the table ready."

Smythe hurried out of the lab and returned shortly leading a fat hog.

Llewellyn said, "Hold it still while I get it strapped into the harness."

After a few minutes of squealing protests, they had struggled, pulled, and fastened the ropes and pulley system that would be used to raise the beast.

"Okay, let the water out of the reservoir," Llewellyn said.

"Right, and I'll add two more lumps of coal to the stove."

"Good show." Llewellyn looked at his pocket watch. "Ten minutes to go. Hit the bellows—now!"

Smythe did as Llewellyn asked, and the flames blasted out of the front of the stove.

"Six minutes, thirty seconds." Llewellyn yelled over the rumbling of the machine.

Smythe grabbed an apple off a small table next to the stove and walked over to the hog. He cut the apple in two and gave one half to the animal.

"Two minutes, twenty seconds."

Dr. Smythe took a small vial of purple powder out of his vest pocket. "Let's see if this is as powerful as they claim." He sprinkled the powder on the other half of the apple.

"One minute, ten seconds."

Smythe gave the powder-coated apple half to the hog, who greedily swallowed it and looked up for more. Suddenly, the animal's eyes rolled up in its head as it dropped dead. The ropes and pulleys squealed in protest as it fell.

"Where's the release valve's whistle?" Smythe said.

"No time to worry about that now. Man the rope."

Smythe grabbed the rope attached to the hog's harness, and he pulled it with all his might. The pulley, and support beam it was attached to, rattled with the weight of the animal's corpse. Once it was four feet off the ground, Dr. Llewellyn swung it on the laboratory table as Smythe released the rope.

"Still no whistle?"

"Damn, the coal must be moist. Add more quickly, and I'll open the chest cavity."

When Smythe finished stoking the fire, he walked back to Dr. Llewellyn, who'd opened the hog's chest and removed the heart.

"Go ahead and connect the tubes to the ascending and descending aortas, and I'll check out that release valve." Llewellyn said, tossing the heart aside.

Smythe quickly attached the circulatory tubes and fastened them with clamps they'd made just for this reason. "Ready here."

Llewellyn walked over, picked up a little hammer, and started to tap on the side of the valve. When he did, it cracked and sent a blast of steam towards his face. He panicked and fell backwards, reaching out wildly for anything to break his fall. He found it when his hand grabbed the lever that controlled the steam's output, pulling it to full power.

The machine began to pulsate as the spring-loaded diaphragm opened and closed.

Thump-THUMP. Thump-THUMP. Thump-THUMP.

The sound grew so loud, Llewellyn began to worry about disturbing the neighbors, but when they heard a loud screech over the throbbing of the artificial heart, Smythe hurried to try to turn off the machine. Before he could deactivate it, the hog's chest exploded. Chunks of swine flesh flew in every direction, amongst a shower of blood.

A soft hiss came from what was left of the creature's corpse, as the sound of the machine slowly grew softer and slower until it finally faded away.

Llewellyn looked at Smythe, who had half a lung lying on top of his head. "I think we woke the neighbors."

They both stopped to listen for any stirring, anything that would explain the screech they'd heard, but they perceived nothing out of the ordinary. After a silent moment, Llewellyn said, "Maybe not?"

"Wonderful, let's try it again."

But Llewellyn stopped him. "We need another hog. Why don't you get one, and I'll replace the release valve and make some adjustments."

"But where can I get one at this hour?"

Llewellyn thought a moment. "The butcher down the street keeps hogs behind his shop; it's where I bought this one. Leave some money and a note on his door and bring one back. But you might want to clean up first," he added, eyeing the blood-splattered Smythe.

A quick scrub later, Smythe was walking a huge hog down the cobblestones on a leash, hoping no one noticed him. The streets were empty, and he made it back to the laboratory without incident, but on his return, he was distressed to find three police officers disembarking their carriage in front of his building. He tried to move nonchalantly into his apartment without attracting notice, but one of the officers spotted him.

In a thick Cockney accent, the first policeman said, "Morning, guv'ner. Sorry to 'old you up, but we received a report of a scream coming from this building. Do you live 'ere?"

"I do, but—um—my pregnant wife had a sudden craving for—for—for bacon. I've been out most of the night searching for—uh—this." He gestured at the hog.

"Eh?" the bobby said. "A little louder, I'm deaf in this ear."

Smythe repeated impatiently what he'd said, and the officer said in his cadenced style, "Would you 'appen to know anyone else living in the apartment that might be available?"

Conjuring up what little he knew about his neighbors, he told the police officer, "I believe there's an old man who lives next door. And I heard he took on a young boarder about a week ago. They may have some information for you."

"'Preciate it, sir. Good luck with the wife. I know what them cravings is like." He looked closely at the doctor for a moment. "Sorry, guv, but you got a little somethin' on your ear."

The doctor reached up, rubbed his ear, and was horrified to see dried, blackened blood on his fingertips.

"Er—just a little mud from the pigpen, I sup-

pose. Guess I had better tidy up before I see the wife. Thanks for the help."

The police officer nodded and went back to his coworkers. Smythe hurried through his door. Tying the hog in place, he told his compatriot what the bobby had said.

"Perhaps we should wait to try again?" Llewellyn asked.

"Wait? Why would we wait?" asked Smythe. "We obviously didn't wake anyone—that scream did. Let's not postpone this test any longer."

Llewellyn sighed but went about resetting the experiment. Once they were sure everything was in place, they turned on the machine once again. It heated up, and before long, blood pumped through its innards. Once more, the apparatus began pulsating, quietly at first, but building in intensity.

Thump-THUMP. Thump-THUMP. Thump-THUMP.

Soon, the noise became near deafening, but the synthetic heartbeat captivated both doctors so much that they didn't notice the volume until they heard yelling coming from next door. Llewellyn crossed to the control board and slid the lever to the "off" position, and the thumping slowed and quieted. When the thumping finally died, Smythe asked, "Did you hear that?"

They listened, but all was silent. Llewellyn went to the window and looked outside. "No movement. I think we're okay."

Smythe gave his colleague an excited smile. "It works! We've created the first artificial heart."

The enthusiasm was contagious, and Llewellyn's otherwise calm facade began to crack. "Yes, and if we can do this with steam, imagine what else we could create. This could be the beginning of a Steam Revolution."

The two men hugged and danced like little boys on Christmas Day. Smythe said, "Let's go celebrate over a pint at the pub."

They went out the front door, but the sight that met them on the other side of the doorway sobered them instantly. The three police officers were hauling out a wild-eyed young man in handcuffs.

As his coworkers took the shackled man to their carriage, the bobby who spoke to Smythe earlier veered over to the two doctors.

"Thanks for the tip. You'll never believe what we discovered."

"What?" asked Smythe, trying to remember what "tip" he'd given the officer.

"We questioned that young man about the yelling, but 'e said it was 'im screaming when 'e woke from a nightmare. We inquired about the old man, but 'e told us his landlord was visiting the country. We searched the apartment but found nothing out of the ordinary and were about to leave when the strangest thing 'appened…" He trailed off at the thought.

"Tell us," Smythe said brusquely. "What happened next?"

"Well, 'e began to pace nervously and got more agitated the longer we stayed until, without warning, 'e screamed and pulled up the planks in the floor. Under the wood was the body of the old man—freshly killed and dismembered."

The doctors gasped, turning pale. Llewellyn managed, "Why did he give himself up?"

"Funniest thing—the young man told us 'e 'eard the 'eartbeat of the old man, growing louder by the second. With my deaf ear, I didn't hear nothin'. My partners said they might've 'eard somethin', but the bloke wouldn't be quiet, so they wasn't sure. But I don't think there was no noise. "

"Why's that?" asked Smythe in barely a whisper.

"Eight days from room letting to bloodletting? I think 'is guilt and shame at his bloodthirsty and cowardly act caused him to imagine it. A dead man's 'eartbeat? Not bloody likely. Pardon my language, guv'ner, but I bet 'e just 'ad a guilty conscience."

The bobby bid them farewell and went to assist the other officer. Within the police carriage, the young man was talking to himself.

"True! Nervous, very dreadfully nervous I had been…"

His voice faded as the carriage drove away.

The Warm Machine

Listen to the clicking of the warm machine.
   Mechanical taps
sound off hours as you grudgingly grow from
   tiny to small.

Maternal hum cocoons you—just listen to that
   contemporary lullaby
composed by exhausted engineers, the same
   engineers who boasted

when they solved ventilation issues or trouble-
   shot error messages.
Engineers devised a bed for you, but roaming
   nurses, who stop

to adjust this knob and that wire, they made
   the bed you lie in.
Nurses with carefully pinned caps and sensible
   shades of lipstick,

those nurses folded delicate bed sheets into
   origami wonders—
little planes, little buses, little trains, little rockets—
   and agonized

over which will carry you to your dreams.
   The head nurse
turns her nurse head, so the others can playfully
   adorn your sailboat

with nail polish emblems to bring good fortune.
   The nurses
can't touch you. This is all they can do for you.
   The warm machine

is your mother now. You breathe her breaths,
   kneed her control
panel breasts. She hums to you, and you hum
   her own song

to her. When the engineers get drunk after work,
   they wonder why
it's not the clicking you mimic. The nurses sigh.
   They don't want to know.

— Alexandra de Romen

High Maintenance

Story by
Vaughn Wright

Illustration by
Laura Givens

For Dano Elliot

When the dead started coming back to life and feeding on the brains of the living, who in turn died and kept the wheel turning, I doubt if anyone was very surprised. For generations before we ever started living in this 24/7 "Thriller" video, we watched the movies and read the novels and did the dances.

It wasn't like when the towers went down, a disaster that turned out to be a singular moment of witness for you and everybody you knew. No, this came in bits and pieces—rumors, suspect video, unconfirmed sources.

Later "official" reports weren't much better. They said it was contained in one place, then said, no, it's contained over here, until eventually it'd gotten everywhere. Leastways, that's how it seemed before the Net and TV and cells and radio went out eight months ago. That's when the law left Dodge, and the only morality that remains is what we've each chosen to accept for ourselves. So how it all started, who's responsible, how it got so far out of hand is a puzzle I doubt we'll ever be able to put together, though word has it there's a gang of scientists somewhere working on a cure. My money's on it coming too late to make a bit of difference.

I know it's already too late for me, because I've got five Michael Jacksons closing in on me and eight bullets left. Normally the math would work in my favor. Problem is, my pistol just jammed. So now I'm standing here with a semi-automatic paperweight in my right hand and my left balled into a fist, thinking I could put 'em to better use by gripping a butt cheek apiece and kissing my black ass good-bye.

"Get down!"

Huh?

"Hit the dirt, you dumbass, and cover your face!"

Important survival tip: When someone barks a command like that in your vicinity, you don't look to see who said it or why; you do like they say and be quick about it. I make like road kill.

BLAM! Click-clack. BLAM! Click-clack. BLAM! Click-clack. BLAM! Click-clack. BLAM! Click-clack.

I love the sound of shotgun in the afternoon.

"You're clear," that stern voice says.

I unfold my arms from atop my head, spit some grass out. The only person standing is a light-skinned brother dressed in black fatigues holding a smoldering pump-action shotgun with a pistol grip. He lifts the clear plastic visor of his riot helmet.

"Looked like you needed a hand," he says, replacing the shells he just spent.

I stand, brush the grass off. "Nah. Had 'em

right where I wanted 'em." I step to my savior with an offered hand. "Good lookin' out. I'm Moe."

He shifts the weapon to his left and points it toward the turf. The double pump he gives me is firm, dry, steady. "Griff."

He's a few inches taller than me, six-foot, six-one, brawny. One of those high-yella pretty boys puts you on your guard if he's in the same room with your girlfriend. I take him to be thirty or a weary twenty-five. Either way, I figure us about the same age.

We survey our handiwork. Seven bodies of mixed races, genders, and ages in varying states of decay lay sprawled on the lawn. I know which two are mine because they only have chunks of their heads missing. Griff's are the ones missing everything from the neck up.

He asks me, "How'd you let yourself get hemmed up like that?"

"I was making my way to the radio station there," I say, a nod toward the little one-story brick building at the end of the walkway, blazing white letters on its roof declaring it to be WEMV. "For the past mile or so it seemed the closer I got, the more company I picked up. I was doing pretty good until this piece of shit crapped out on me."

Griff takes my handgun, looks it over. "You only have the one?" he asks me in a way that says he's curious why those brain biters were after me in the first place; my picnic basket is empty.

Griff, on the other hand, defines armed and dangerous. The guy is a walking arsenal. Aside from the shotgun, I see an assault rifle slung over his back, twin laser-sighted .45s in a dual shoulder rig; a really big nickel-plated revolver on his right hip, a machete on the left. The utility pockets of his pants are bulging with ammunition. Whatever girlfriend Griff wants, he's gonna get.

"If you'd waited another minute," I tell him, "I would've threatened to beat them with my belt."

Griff chuckles, then returns my gun and asks me where I'm from.

"Camden," I say, thinking how it seems half a world away now rather than just across the Delaware River. "There were ten of us when we decided to try to get with a bigger group, somewhere safer. Some said New York; some said Philly. With all the people in New York, you gotta figure you'd do so much shootin', your trigger finger would catch a cramp. Me and my crew went with Philly because it's closer and we'd likely have some bullets left over after we got here.

"So day before yesterday the four of us came

across the Ben Franklin Bridge. As soon as we hit the city, we picked up a couple more guys. One of the Philly dudes told us about this DJ named Mark B doin' live daily broadcasts from WEMV, down here in Southwest. He said he and his buddy didn't much care for the odds of just the two of them makin' the trip crosstown, but since we showed up we should give it a go together, so we started making our way here.

"I'm the only one left" I say funereally. "Somehow, everybody turned Michael Jackson without anybody ever gettin' bit."

Griff creases his brow in puzzlement. "Fouled water supply?"

I shake my head and tell him, "Couldn't've been. I drank the same water as everybody else."

"Any skirmishes on the way?"

"A few, never more than a couple of M.J.s here and there."

"Well, Thriller isn't airborne. You don't just *get* it, not without an exchange of bodily fluids," Griff explains, like I don't know this already. "More than likely the infections came from your conflicts on the way here. Shoot those things at close range, whack 'em in the head, cut an arm off, blood goes everywhere. All you need is a drop in your eyes or mouth and you're done." Griff lowers his visor. It's dotted with minute speckles of blood. "See what I mean?"

Yeah, and it gives me a serious chill. I've got 317 kills. It's a wonder I've survived so long.

He says, "I take it you could use a meal and some rest."

I grin. "Griff, you're startin' to be my best friend."

"Well, you're welcome to come, but first you're gonna have to strip."

"Say what?"

Griff takes two steps back, snaps his face shield down, raises his shotgun until it's centered on my chest. "Moe, if you've got anything that looks like a bite mark on you, you're done. Right here, right now. Don't like it, the highway's right there behind you."

"I can tell you now, I haven't been bitten," I say with my hands where he can see them. "Only, how do you know I didn't *just* get infected by gettin' some blood in my eye or something?"

"That type of infection takes at least four hours. By then, you'll be fed, rested, and on your way."

"What about Mark B? He's the one I came here to see."

"Strip or leave."

I'm tired, hungry, and unarmed. Takes me about ten seconds to peel out of my t-shirt, jeans, and

boots. He lets me keep my dignity on. After certifying me USDA, Griff says we have to bury the bodies.

"Griff, I'm *tired*, man. Let 'em rot."

"You see that building there?" he asks me, pointing at the nearest residential structure. A seven-story apartment building. "That's where I live. Rotting corpses stink, promote disease, and make the area look blighted."

"Seriously, dude, property values ain't what they're cracked up to be anymore."

Despite my grumbling, I still follow Griff around to the back of the station, where there's a little grounds keeping shed with some shovels and picks and work gloves.

We find a clear spot in the woods back there shaded from the May sun by the surrounding trees and start digging. With his helmet off, I see his hair is in six perfect cornrows that furrow back to the nape of his neck and end in rubber bands. Pretty boy, definitely. I'll give him his props though. I try to keep up, but the guy is a shoveling machine, really throws his back into it. Still, it takes us working the afternoon through before the hole is deep enough to pile everybody in. All the while, I don't have a lot to say. I'm kinda pissed about having to bury these cranium crunchers.

After we drag the M.J.s around and cover them over, neither of us have any words to say over them. I can't speak for Griff, but I believe in God. Always will. But for a long time now I've been of the mind that prayers won't mean jack this late in the game for the twice dead.

When we head for his apartment building we're both grimy messes. Griff promises a hot shower and a change of clothes.

We go in through a rear maintenance entrance Griff says is the only point of entry that isn't bricked over from the inside. Once the steel door is locked behind us, he uses a high-powered pocket flashlight to lead me along a maintenance passageway, then up the service stairs.

At the landing between the third and fourth floors he cautions me to step over a tripwire for the fifth time. Griff is not playing about his booby traps. What won't impale, decapitate, or flame broil an intruder, will turn him and anybody within a ten-foot blast radius of him into a fine red mist. This time I curiously trace the nearly invisible fishing line back to a corner, and then up to a V-8 engine block. It's just dangling there over our heads. How the hell he got it up there, I don't ask. I'm just glad I'm an invited guest and keep it moving.

On the fourth floor, we leave the stairwell. An outer window on the building's western side has the hall full of setting sun. It gives a nice glow, a living warmth, to a place that feels like a massive mausoleum.

We stop in front of apartment 4-G. Inside, I notice right away how cool it is. Too cool.

Incredulous, I ask Griff, "You got A/C?"

"Yeah," he says. "I keep a generator going up on the seventh floor for this place and a couple over at the station."

He hits a wall switch that turns on lamps in the living room and a ceiling fixture above a dining area just off of it. Straight back is an unlit hallway with at least three doors, all closed.

He offers me a seat at a glass-top dining table, which I nearly collapse in. Even after he stows his arsenal in a closet behind the first hallway door, he still has the revolver strapped to his thigh and the machete on his belt. I suppose it's his leisure wear.

"I'm a sandwich guy," he informs me. "Bake the bread myself. Roast beef all right with you?"

"Hey, whatever's clever, Griff, as long as it's *dead*."

While he's hooking me up in the kitchen, I scope out the crib, wondering if this is his original home or simply some place he's conveniently squatted. It's furnished nice, lots of glass and chrome. Plush black leather sectional and matching lounge chair. Some mirrored prints on the walls. Big flatscreen over a high-end entertainment system. Between that and an adjoining wall with heavy drapes I figure cover sliding glass doors is what looks like a ham radio, with headphones and a handheld microphone sitting next to it.

I'm over there, curiously checking it out, when Griff comes from around the corner of the kitchen. He sets a bottle of beer and a plate with two sandwiches on it on the table where I'd been sitting.

"That's a remote setup for the radio station," he tells me, then clears his throat and, with a Barry White husk to his voice, goes, "This is Mark B, comin' at you live from WEMV."

"You … you're him?" I say, more surprised than I guess I ought to be. "That's why I came here. He, you said there was a Thriller-free sanctuary somewhere, right?"

"I'm gonna tell you the truth, Moe: If there's a safe place, I couldn't tell you where it is. I honestly don't believe one even exists anymore. I'm sure some of the government types have a bunker somewhere, and somebody's using that hole in the ground bin Laden hid out in all those years, but stiffs like you and me, we're on our own."

He leads me over to the balcony, draws back the drapes. Our view from four stories up is ideally vantaged to overlook the squat brick structure of WEMV. And, yeah, I'll admit it's a much pleasanter sight without a bunch of rotting-flesh lawn ornaments laying helter-skelter in front of it.

Griff says, "I can see anyone approaching, how many, how they're armed, or, in a case like yours, if they're bringing trouble with them. I don't like what I see, I let 'em go on about their business. Don't get too many of those though."

"But if there's no sanctuary, why tell people there is?"

Griff looks me squarely in the eyes, and says, "You ever been in love, Moe?"

"Sure," I say, wondering how that left turn in the conversation happened.

I follow him back over to the table and retake my seat. The sandwiches are each about two inches thick. The beer is ice cold. I'm *really* liking this guy.

He sits across from me and says, "Of course you have. How could you not. Everyone has or had someone. Someone who made you feel like your whole existence had been validated the moment you first met 'em. Seeing their face or hearing their voice never failed to send every particle of your being into overdrive with yearning. You can't turn it off. You know if you live to be a hundred, the desire'll never die."

While I start chowing down, he methodically unrolls an oilcloth full of tools I recognize as used for working on firearms. He asks for my gun. I hand it to him. He's very adept with the pistol, has it in pieces on the table in no time.

"I know exactly what you mean," I say, nodding, thinking of Tamara Spruill.

Me and Tamara went to high school together. Man, I had it bad. Every time I saw her, my teenage hormones sent my heart into palpitations and locked my lungs up, not to mention dropped my I.Q. about 30 points. My parents thought I needed a twelve-step program. I was too chickenshit to ever try to get close to her. Ten years later, I wouldn't care if she gained fifty pounds, was baldheaded and had a mustache—if she told me to jump, I'd still ask her what flavor moon cheese she wants.

Griff grins in a way that says he's peeped the wistful longing in my eyes. "So you at least understand that's how it was with me and Kanara Knox."

"Kanara Knox?" Who wourdn't. Face of an angel, body like a dream, voice as sweet as a summer breeze. Though, me, I prefer girls in the hood. Celebrity broads, they're nice to look at and all, but I always try to keep my fantasies in the realm of possibility. "Did you know her?"

"All my life. We grew up together, used to live in the same apartment building."

Griff shifts in his seat to pull out a black leather wallet. He flips it open and hands it to me. Sure enough, there's him and Kanara cheesing it up in one of those photo booths. I look across the table at him, then at the picture again. His eyes have a haunted quality now that we all have these days and he's lost some weight, but the picture is fairly recent. Duly impressed, I hand the wallet back.

Griff studies the flick for a moment, obviously as caught up in something he can't get back as I was a minute ago, before he closes the billfold and with it his eyes. He sighs, repockets the wallet.

"So, what," I ask him, "you were bangin' that?"

"No, nothing like that," Griff says without a trace of defensiveness. "Guys like you and me, Moe, we don't have our dreams come true. Not ever. It just doesn't happen. Might get something close, but never the way we expect."

He tosses me the round that had lodged in my gun, a souvenir.

"Me and Kay-Kay were close, friends," he says, "but it never got romantic between us. There just wasn't that two-way chemistry, you know what I mean? She knew how I felt though.

"I'll tell you one thing about Kay-Kay, she was real people. Never too busy to help a friend or too proud to accept some if she needed it. Like when she was with that rap guy—"

"Slinkie Slim," I interrupt, starting on my second sandwich, recalling what I picked up from a tabloid.

"His name was Emanuel," he drolly informs me, starting to do the reassembly. "I warned her the guy was gonna dog her out. I didn't say it because I was trying to clear the field for myself. I just didn't want to see somebody I cared about getting hurt, you know?"

I nod, because I do.

"When she broke off their engagement after finding out about all the running around he was doing on her, I never played the I-told-you-so card, just gave her my shoulder to cry on until she got herself together enough to make another movie. That's what she was doing when Thriller popped up on us."

I down some beer, and say, "You were with her?"

"Not until after she came home to be with her family. By then her parents, brother and sisters, and a lot of our neighbors were already moon walkin'."

"Damn."

"Yeah, but she found me and we took to riding things out together. We'd both lost everybody else, so we were pretty much all each other had at that point. We were already the best of friends, but being sort of sole survivors in a crazy world where it seemed everybody'd just escaped from an asylum, Moe, it was like living a special kind of high. I mean, every minute of every day we knew could be our last, but we were surviving them together. Just me and her. Can you dig that?"

"Like dirt," I say, and mean it.

"But even then I knew something'd go wrong."

The interest in my eyes urges him on.

"I'd always hoped that if either us ever got infected, it'd be me. It'd be hard on her, sure, but she'd bounce back from it eventually. If she went first, I knew I'd go right out the side door. I'm talkin' fourteen-karat crazy, Moe. And I'm gonna tell you," he looks at me narrowly, "that's right where I am today.

"It was the end of November, about two months after the blackout." When the power grids failed, he means. "Up until then, we'd been spending a lot of time cooped up indoors. I rarely let her go out, because I could move faster alone when I went scavenging. Only it was snowing that day, the first snow since Thriller, and Kay, she just wanted to be out in the stuff. Wanted to throw some snowballs or some shit. I didn't care. With me, it was whatever she wanted. So we go.

"It was nice, real quiet, peaceful, you know? And Kay-Kay never looked more lovely. A flush had risen up in her cheeks from the cold, and some snowflakes got caught in those long lashes of hers. Maybe it was me being so caught up in just being with her, or maybe it was the snow that made it real easy for one of those things to creep us on the q.t. Maybe it was both. But before I knew it, one of 'em had gotten so close it was within arm's reach of Kay-Kay before I saw it. I raised my gun and shouted for her to run, but you know reflexes; she turned to see what the danger was just as I fired, and ended up with a face full of blow-back blood."

My jaw nearly bangs the table.

"Yeah," he says tightly, seeing my reaction. "Neither one of us knew that was a way to get infected back then." He shakes his head. "We both thought she'd be okay … until she wasn't."

Griff falls silent for a bit as his hands finish doing work they can seemingly do without any conscious help from him. I sip my beer, not the least bit envious of him. It would rip my insides to shreds if I saw Tamara turn Michael Jackson and then had to put her down, especially if I felt responsible for it.

Presently, Griff declares my gun, "Right as rain." He slaps a magazine into its handle, racks a round into the chamber, and says, "We oughta test it first though, just to make sure."

"Knock yourself out," I say, because I figure if I've ever met anyone who knows how to certify a weapon, it's him.

Actually, with my belly full, my mind's on that hot shower now. Only the next thing Griff does is swing the gun under the table. I see through the glass top that it's pointed at my left leg and—*blam!*—my kneecap gets blown to smithereens"

The pain, the pain … listen, you've *never* had pain like this. I fall to the floor, writhing in agony, cussing and screaming and holding what's left of my knee, feeling the bone fragments grinding around in there, the searing heat.

As for Griff, it's like he's already forgotten he just crippled the shit out of me. His gaze is fixed on something down the unlit hallway behind me. Someone else is here? I crane my head around.

Through tears and lightning bolts of pain I try to focus on the figure emerging from the darkness of a back room. It gradually shambles into the light in that unsteady Thriller gait. The figure is distinctly feminine—petite—in a yellow summer dress. Her milk chocolate complexion is mottled. Face slack. Drool dribbles from the left corner of her gaping mouth. And yet she has a fresh do, brightly painted nails, rouged cheeks. Her expensive perfume has a putrid bottom scent.

The gunshot must have been her dinner bell.

Between what I figure's been regular feeding and refrigeration, Griff's done a good job of keeping her up. Even six-months living dead, there's still some beauty to be found in Kanara Knox. Just don't look for it in her vacant, soulless eyes.

Griff finally gives me his gaze back. He has the same kind of sad, almost apologetic expression on his face I'd probably have if I were in his place.

Lamia
For Clark Ashton Smith

She has seen the Yellow Sign
wax golden in the final throes
and knows the usages of venom
gone honeyed on the tongue.
All hungers are succored at her pores
but from her lips the breath of time
flows to an abhorrent design—
not mine, nor yours, nor any creature's
whose logic lives under an orange sun
and weaves a patterned web
across the runnels of decay.
Spawn of the midnight
that's uncertain of a dawn,
bone of amaranth visions
and flesh of languorous lies,
she can entice the fingertips
to lush worlds and austere.
But I have seen those odalisques' thighs
with eyes that terror made lucid
and shorn of the habiliments of desire
she inspires only parodies of wonder,
threnodies of fear.
Yet even now, when the wind soughs
through the cypresses
and I hear her keening
by the doors of crumbling mausoleums,
the skin along my spine grows taut.
What can she yearn for
beyond the gate of Yog-Sothoth
and why do I crave to follow
past realms and times
distraught and hollow
through formula and incantation
to the central core, inchoate…
that horrid source and seed of chaos
where, perhaps, some formless, long-forgotten
    question
swarms within its answer, unasked, unheralded,
    unsought?

— Karin L. Frank

First appeared in *Transcendental Tales*, 2006.

Black Orchid

Story by Rick Novy
Illustration by Jag Lall

When Maricel came out of the building, I didn't recognize her at first. She held her head low, and raven hair hid her face from view. She dressed the way most musicians would for an audition, dark and formal. I finally recognized the small flute case she carried in her right hand.

I gave the horn a quick burst and she looked up. When she saw the car, she jogged over and got inside. She had been crying; I could tell by the way the makeup ran from her eyes down her cheek. The audition couldn't have gone well. I decided not to ask, but she told me anyway.

"I couldn't concentrate." She breathed in through her teeth then blew the breath through pursed lips. "I knew this would happen. Who sent it?"

The "it" she meant was a black orchid we found on the front porch this morning. When it arrived, Maricel couldn't contain herself. She had been practicing for her audition, but the black orchid threw her out of the zone to the point she couldn't remember a piece she had been studying for months.

"Why did it have to come today?" She buried her head in her hands and began to cry. "Of all days, today. Somebody is trying to sabotage my career before it is even started."

I should know better than to argue with Maricel when she got an idea into her head. But I tried anyway. I had to try because she struggled enough with depression at Juilliard.

I started the car and shifted into gear. "Nobody is trying to sabotage your career."

She spat an evil look in my direction. "Why did it show up? And why today? And why black?" She smacked her flute case with her fist.

"Be careful, you still have another audition." Freezing up because something got into her head he could understand. Not auditioning at all because she broke her flute in a fit of rage, he could not.

"Like I have a chance." She slumped in her seat.

She wouldn't if she kept up that attitude, but I didn't say anything. I just concentrated on driving back to the house.

The flat tire happened on route 237. We rent a farm about twenty miles outside the city limits. Even after we reach the freeway exit, there's another five miles of two-lane highway to navigate, and it's rarely traveled.

Gravel on the shoulder crunched as I pulled off to the side of the road. Of course, the flat did nothing but upset Maricel even more. I wanted to say something, but instead I sat there staring at her cheek. I couldn't think of anything that would make the situation better. In the end, I just got out of the car and made my way back to the trunk.

As I pulled out the jack, I brooded on Maricel's mental state. I really thought she could pull it together for these auditions. Sometimes I let Maricel's depression get to me. She mopes and scolds herself and it brings me down with her.

She hadn't said anything to me since before we got onto the interstate. All during the time I removed the flat tire, I tried thinking of something—anything—to bring Maricel out of her funk. She hadn't even bothered to get out of the car until I had the tire removed.

She hung her feet out the door and dropped to the ground. Without even a glance in my direction, she walked across the highway and stood with her back to me. She did that sort of thing at home, too, hiding in a closet or disappearing under the bed. Other times she would just sit and stare into space.

I just sighed and pulled the spare from the trunk. The tire felt a little under-inflated, but would get us home. I changed the tire, sweat dripped down my forehead, burning when it ran into my eye. I wiped it away using the shoulder of my t-shirt.

By the time I finished tightening the last lug nut, I expected her to be feeling better, but she hadn't moved. She still stood with her back to the car, and I couldn't tell what had such a tight grip on her attention. I shouted to her across the street. "I'm almost done. Just have to drop the car and put the jack away."

Not even a flinch for a response. I hadn't seen her this bad for a long time, and could only shake my head and finish what I had to do.

The scream came as the car settled on the ground and I picked up the jack. The scream had a shrill tone to it, not a scream of anger but of terror. I leapt to my feet and looked over the top of the car to see Maricel sprinting toward me. Behind her, a completely opaque, black, amorphous thing followed—a thing like nothing I had ever seen before.

It slithered up the shoulder on the far side of the road, seemingly without any thickness at all, like a blot of nothing that moved toward the car. I could feel my breathing get quicker as Maricel ran around the front. I opened the door and threw the jack into the back seat, then I ran around the back of the car, hoping to get into the driver's seat before the thing got there first. Lord only knew what might happen if it touched me.

Fortunately, it didn't move very fast. I got in while it still had another six feet of ground to cover. Maricel sat bug-eyed in the passenger seat, panting as if she had finished a footrace, which I suppose in some sense, she had. I know, my own heart kept thumping against my breastbone.

She kept looking out my window. "Start the car."

Just then, I realized that I got in so quickly I never had time to fish the keys out of my pocket. I fumbled around with my hand, trying to dig them out of the front pocket of my blue-jeans while sitting down. Not an easy task, but I finally managed to get them out.

The black thing started climbing my door and I quickly pulled my elbow inside. The key went into the ignition with great difficulty, but I finally got the car started despite my shaking hands. As the black thing began pouring in through my window, I stepped on the gas and momentum peeled it away.

We left the blob in the middle of the road, but on my lap I discovered another black orchid. Maricel snatched it off my lap before I had a chance to take a hand off the steering wheel. The orchid zipped past my face as she hurled it out the window on my side. The whole incident left Maricel trembling, and neither of us spoke the rest of the trip home.

When we did get back to the old farmhouse, I pulled the car into my normal spot underneath the giant elm. I shut off the engine and got out, but Maricel didn't move. After walking around the front of the car, I rapped on the passenger window. She still wouldn't move.

She locked the door so it wouldn't open. Now, the black thing still had me a bit freaked out, but it left her petrified. "Come on, Maricel. Let's go inside."

She moved her head ever so slightly so she could see my face from the corner of her eye, but she didn't speak.

I had to use the key to open the door and pull her out. She didn't resist, but neither did she help. In fact, her arm felt limp and lifeless as we walked to the house.

Once inside, I led her to the kitchen table and she collapsed into her usual chair. I brought her a glass of cold lemonade. After ten minutes, beads of condensation ran down the sides of the glass to leave a wet ring on the table, undisturbed because Maricel never touched the glass.

I waited another ten minutes before I realized she left her flute in the car. I ran outside to get it and returned to find her lemonade in the center of the table. A wet streak showed the path along which she pushed away the glass.

I set her flute case on the table near the streak. Maricel picked it up and moved it away from the water, proving that she did still care about something. It gave me a little spark to work with.

With a symphonic audition in under twenty-four hours, I had to bring Maricel back to life and put the music back into her fingers. "Why don't you try to practice for tomorrow's audition?"

Maricel pushed the flute case a little bit farther away. Exasperated, I went out to the barn to do something else for a while. Maybe I could get that old tractor running—anything to give my mind a break from Maricel's toxic state. Getting her out of my mind was not so easy, however.

As I slid open the door to the old barn, the tang of nitrogen-rich fertilizer almost overwhelmed me. The lights dangling from the ceiling turned on with a switch in an exposed box nailed on the open studs. Bare conduit led from the box up to the lights, which didn't add much illumination over what the sun brought through the door.

Bags of fertilizer on the other side of the barn hid most of a green and yellow tractor. From the door, I could only see the nose of it. It had been left behind by the landlord who told me he was too old to farm anymore. I had tried half-heartedly to get it started in the past, but couldn't get the engine to turn over.

I came out here to get my mind off of Maricel, but she crept back into it as I walked across the barn. Whatever the result of tomorrow's audition, I would have live with it. I tried to get the whole situation out of my mind as I climbed onto the seat of the tractor, but the thoughts wouldn't stay out until I got elbow-deep into the engine.

It took me only a few minutes to isolate the problem with the tractor to the spark plugs. It took over an hour to find replacements. I finally found spares under some bags of fertilizer and swapped the plugs out.

I thought I'd drive the tractor to the front door and surprise Maricel. Maybe a ride would help her to feel better. I drove it out of the barn and onto the gravel driveway, engine rumbling and shaking the seat. When I got outside, I couldn't believe my eyes. Coming off the road at the end of the driveway, that same flat black blob we left a few miles up the road eased its way toward the farmhouse.

I felt a bead of sweat roll down my back as I

raced to cut it off. I couldn't let it get to Maricel. If I could stop the tractor on top of the blob, maybe the thing would be pinned long enough to get the sheriff out here to deal with it. After the stories he told about the Gulf War, the sheriff would know what to do here.

I gunned the engine and despite my better judgment and trembling knees, I headed directly at the thing. I don't know if it saw me because I don't think it had any eyes, but it did seem to sense me in some way. An abrupt change of direction proved that, but it couldn't outrun the tractor.

When I caught up, I drove right over the top of the blob and stopped with the big wheels at the center. I leapt across the body of the creature and landed on the gravel driveway, rolling to break the momentum.

From my hands and knees, I watched in amazement as the blob simply slithered around the tire and continued flowing its way toward the front door.

Inside, Maricel must have regained her composure. Just as the thing passed the front picture window I heard a C Major scale. It's the way she warmed up on flute. She worked the Circle of Fifths, starting with C Major and working around in the sharp direction until she finished with F Major on the flat side.

The sound of the flute caused the creature to waver. It shuddered and stopped its progress, as if listening to the pure tone from Maricel's instrument. If I had a way to capture the blob, it would have been an easy target just then. Problem was, if it could flow around the tire of a tractor parked on top of it, most likely it could flow through my arms if I grabbed at it.

When Maricel stopped playing after she finished her warm-up, the creature advanced toward the front porch again. It flowed up the three steps and dropped something at the top. Maricel started playing arpeggios and the thing sank into the ground, vanishing without a trace.

Left behind at the top of the three porch steps, a black orchid, lying with the flower toward me and the stem pointed away. The sound of Maricel's arpeggios still drifted through the walls. I couldn't let her know about this encounter. Nothing could be more important to her than the next audition.

I sat down on the top step and picked up the black orchid. I didn't really have a chance to take a close look at one until now.

Rolling it over and over in my hands, I inspected the leaves and the petals of the black orchid. I could see nothing to indicate it anything other than a true black orchid. I didn't even know such a thing

existed until the one we found yesterday arrived. I wondered whether this one occurred in nature, or if somehow a white orchid had been dyed.

Maricel began playing the audition piece she needed for tomorrow. It didn't seem like a particularly difficult piece, at least not for her. Maybe it had been one of her assignments while at the conservatory. That would explain why it sounded so fluid and effortless.

In fact, she sounded so good on this particular piece, I couldn't imagine anything like what happened during today's audition happening at tomorrow's. On the other hand, she seemed very solid on that piece, too, and she blew it.

I stared down at the black orchid in my hand. I had to get rid of it. The tractor I left in the driveway caught my attention, and I decided to put it back in the barn. I drove the tractor to its spot behind the fertilizer bags and dropped the black orchid between the bags and the wall. If she ever found it there, it would likely be desiccated and crumbling by then.

Since the tractor engine hadn't caused Maricel to miss a beat, I decided to go back inside and listen. She finished her practice session a few minutes later and came into the kitchen to prepare dinner.

She wore a contented look on her face, and that caused me to smile. "You look like you're feeling better."

She looked at me with those perceptive eyes I fell in love with. "You got the tractor working."

She did notice. "Did you see it?" If she had, she might also have seen what else I did.

"No babe, I just heard you driving it around." She disappeared into the pantry.

Nothing much happened that evening. We watched a movie on cable and then went to bed. Not a sign of the black blob thing, black orchids, or a mental breakdown. We went up to bed and Maricel fell right to sleep.

The next morning, I woke up first. I used the opportunity to cook breakfast, and I had it ready by the time Maricel came downstairs. I decided not to speak of the audition she had in a couple hours. If she did want to talk about it, she would have to be the first to mention it.

Before she arose, I even took the opportunity to look outside for any more black orchids. I could only find the one I had dropped behind the fertilizer in the barn. She didn't know about that one, and I had no plan to tell her about it.

She finished her breakfast with a look of contentment, and for the most part, without speaking.

I fell in love with *this* girl, not the one I drove home from the city with yesterday. The black blob hadn't appeared since the previous evening, and while Maricel got dressed for the audition, I went outside to look for it. It would be dreadful if the thing showed up now.

I scanned the gravel up and down the driveway and saw no sign of it. I even looked up the road and saw nothing. When I got back to the porch steps, I kicked the dirt where I saw the thing disappear the last time it showed up. Nothing but dirt. I decided it wasn't around and went back inside.

Maricel walked into the kitchen just as I came back inside. She held her flute case and book bag and looked set to go. "You ready, babe?"

She smiled and gave me a quick nod.

"Let's go." I expected no trouble, and held the door open for her. I locked the door behind us, but as soon as she stepped toward the stairs, the black thing emerged from the ground. It just oozed up like a seeping of blood.

Maricel screamed and began to cry with frantic sobs. The thing started climbing the porch steps, causing Maricel to back into the now-locked door.

I put my arm around her shoulder and pulled her close, but it did not calm her in the least. It didn't calm me, either. The thing blocked our path to the car, and I doubted that we could both leap over it. I might be able to, but Maricel wore a gown and heels. She couldn't jump wearing that, and I wouldn't leave her here alone.

As the thing climbed to the top step, Maricel tried to shrink even further back into the door. Something had to be done. Desperation and panic started to fog my mind. Then it struck me how, yesterday, her scales made the thing pause.

I took the flute case from Maricel and opened it. "Put it together and play."

She gave me a bewildered look and shook her head violently. "I am not going to play flute with this monster coming at me."

I dropped to one knee and set the flute case on the porch. I knew this to be the right thing to do, and I knew how to put the flute together myself. Sort of. I started and Maricel screamed at me. "What are you doing?"

Despite wanting to keep yesterday's visit a secret, I had to tell her what I saw. "This thing was here last night. It appeared just before you started practicing."

Maricel said nothing, but I could see the anger in her eyes. Why didn't I tell her before now? I didn't have time to apologize. The thing was nearly upon us.

"When you started playing scales, it stopped moving, almost as if listening to you."

"What?"

Still on one knee, I lifted the flute over my head. Maricel took it from me and blew an open tone. The thing shuddered, but did not stop.

"You put the head joint on upside-down." I got back to my feet in time to see her rotate it 180 degrees. She lifted the flute to her mouth with the black blob thing only inches from our feet.

Maricel played a C Major scale and the thing stopped. She played the G Major scale and the blob retreated ever-so-slightly. She continued through the circle of fifths and the thing retreated from the porch.

"Keep playing." I pulled the car keys from my pocket and grabbed the flute case from the floor of the porch. When I stood, I put my hand around her waist and guided her to the car. She continued playing, changing from major scales to minor arpeggios.

I opened the car door for her and she got inside. She stopped playing to close the door as I ran to the other side to get into the car myself. When she stopped, the black thing charged at us, moving faster than I thought it could.

I got the car started and shifted into reverse, spraying gravel as I backed out rather abruptly with the thing hanging on Maricel's door. When I shifted out of reverse and stepped on the gas, it lost its grip and fell away.

Only after we had gone three or four miles did she speak. "It's going to happen again. I'm going to stumble on an easy audition piece.

"Put your flute back in the case." I reached over and stroked her hair with my right hand. "Don't you see? You have complete control over it."

She gave me an astonished and bewildered look. "It's stalking me. It wants me to fail."

I put my right hand back on the wheel so I could turn onto the freeway ramp. "But when you play, the thing retreats. It's like some part of your mind doesn't want you to succeed, but if you play with conviction, that part is suppressed and the real musician in you emerges."

"You think this is all in my head?" She looked about ready to hit me with the flute case.

"I don't know if it's in your head because I can see the blob, but that's how it's behaving." I paused to merge with freeway traffic. Once I got into the left lane, I continued. "All you need to do is focus on your playing and the thing should leave you alone."

She sighed and looked at her lap. "I don't know."

"You can do it." She didn't answer me, and we didn't talk the rest of the trip into town.

Maricel considered the yesterday's audition to be for the back-up job. She thought herself a shoe-in for that chair, but when she stumbled, she lost her safety net. Now, she faced the audition for her first choice without a net. What if she stumbled again?

I understood her trepidation completely. An individual failing at something that should be easy really could cause an emotional breakdown. Of that, I was convinced.

After parking the car, I escorted her to the audition room, but they asked me to wait outside. I gave Maricel a peck on the cheek for luck. "Remember, just play with conviction. Play as if you are part of the flute. Never mind anything else." She did not answer me. She just opened the wooden door and disappeared into the room, leaving me to join a small cluster of better-halves.

From the hallway, I could hear the different musicians all playing the same piece Maricel practiced last night. Each sounded good, but none sounded like her. I could always tell Maricel's playing, even during a flute choir. Her attack, and the way she finished her notes—I can't really describe how it sounds, it just sounds like nobody else's playing—on any instrument.

It took another fifteen or twenty minutes before I heard that unique attack, but she played the opening phrases of the piece without flaw. Then I looked at the door and saw the tail end of the black thing disappear underneath. It flowed right around another man's foot to get through.

"Did you see that?"

The man looked at me like I spoke a foreign language. "See what"

"The thing that went off your foot and under the door." I didn't want to be too specific. If the man saw it, he would know what I meant.

But the man apparently didn't see what I had seen. "That cockroach?"

"Is that what it was?" So the man hadn't seen the black thing. I didn't really know what that meant, but it didn't matter as much as what Maricel's reaction would be if she saw the black thing.

But she did see it. I knew when she first spotted the thing because she stumbled over a note she normally had no problem with. I closed my eyes, wishing

it were my ears instead. I didn't want to listen. She would be hell to live with if she blew this audition. But then, something unexpected happened.

Maricel put everything she had into playing that piece. She sounded better than I ever heard her sound before. More conviction, more skill, and more artistry and feeling than she had ever put into her music. It emerged through the door and walls with a flawless precision unmatched by any of the other performers.

The black thing scurried back under the door and tried to make an escape down the hall. The other man lifted his boot and stomped on it, twisting his foot in the process. I looked him in the eye, and he flashed a quick grin.

"See, cockroach."

Where he saw a smashed cockroach, I saw the black thing turning gray. Pretty soon, it dissolved right into the floor.

Through the door, I could hear Maricel end the piece with a flourish. This was the Maricel I fell for. This was the Maricel who expected to win any chair she desired.

She didn't emerge for quite a while, probably another hour. Several more players auditioned during that time. None sounded as good to me as Maricel's attempt. It could have been love, or it could have been that she really did play better. I didn't care which, because Maricel had defeated the black thing. She beamed with confidence as we walked back to the car. She positively radiated the aura of success, even though she wouldn't know the results of the audition until late.

"I think you played well enough to win this chair."

She didn't answer me right away. She just smiled and then turned her head to look out the window. "It doesn't matter. If I don't get this chair, I'll win the next."

That caught me by surprise. It sounded like a Maricel who had slain her demons. When we got back to the farm, on the top step of the porch, we found a white orchid.

The Darkest Part of the Forest

Story by C.J. Killmer
Illustration by Neil T. Foster

I grew up in Florida, but not the real Florida. The real Florida I did not discover until I returned to the Sunshine State after over a decade of absence. After high school, I had wandered far from the sandbar peninsula—first, a traditional liberal arts education at a small college in the Midwest; then, a tour in the army, followed by several years of guiding hunters and fishermen out West. I didn't discover the real Florida until I returned from that exodus.

The occasion of my return was the death of my sole living relative, Uncle Lloyd. His death meant that the sprawling ranch in the north-central region of the state, which I had never visited before, passed to me. I expected that I would stay there for a few months, surely less than a year, just long enough to personally oversee the sale of the land, before returning to my beloved Rockies.

I met my uncle's lawyer, Bob Anderson, at the front gate to the property. He was a gray-haired man in a shirt and tie, sleeves rolled up against the autumn heat. We shook hands. When he spoke, it was in the educated good ol' boy accent of a man who had attended a Southern state university.

"Good to meet you, Ben."

"Likewise," I said.

"Sorry we have to meet again under such circumstances."

I shrugged.

"You didn't know Lloyd well, did you?"

"Never met him, and I only heard a little bit about him when I was growing up."

"Well, long story short, all the land and everything on it's yours. It's a done deal. Here are the keys to the house," he said, handing them to me. "Of course, all the cattle are dead, so if you're planning on keeping the ranch running, you'll have to replace 'em."

"The cattle are dead?"

"Lloyd used to have hundreds of 'em, but they're all gone. Supposedly they all just up and croaked, only a couple days before Lloyd himself checked out."

"Any idea what killed them?"

"No clue. But your uncle's buddy, Sam Kenton, he might know. Sam worked for your uncle, but the two were best friends and were really almost like partners. Sam lives in town. After the cows died, he refused to work on the ranch anymore. Then, a couple days later, Lloyd died. Sam didn't seem the least bit troubled by that—his attitude seemed to be one more of 'I told you so.' Which was surprising

because, like I said, the two guys were great friends, up till the cattle died. If you're still curious, you might try talking to Sam."

He gave me directions to Sam's house. I thanked him and he left.

* * *

Sam lived in a small but well-maintained house near the edge of the nearest town. He was courteous enough, but definitely seemed aloof. I started by asking him about the cattle.

"The cows all died in the same area of Lloyd's property," Sam said.

"Where's that?"

"Same place Lloyd himself died—the darkest part of the forest."

"The forest on the ranch?"

He nodded. "It's mostly pines with palmetto scrub, but there's this one area where it turns into big ol' oaks and cypress, and it's real dark, even on sunny days. It's a scary place."

"How so?"

He shrugged. "Hard to explain, but if you ever go there, you'll see what I mean. There's always been a fence around it, as far back as I can remember, but recently the fence got damaged somehow. That's how the cows got over there. And they all died. Vet couldn't tell us why, but I knew it was something with that spot. Plus, there's the statue."

"Statue?"

"An Indian. I don't really know much about it, how old it is, anything like that. It looks real old. And it's creepy, too. It's right under the biggest, ugliest, scariest-looking oak you ever saw. I think there's some kinda story to that statue, and Lloyd knew what it was, but he wouldn't say. Wouldn't tell me, his best friend. You believe that?"

I shook my head. "Sounds pretty weird."

"You ain't kiddin'. I think that statue's what makes that part of the woods … well, the way it is. Almost like the statue's cursed or something, I don't know. But I'll tell you what, I don't for one second think it's coincidence that Lloyd and the cattle just happened to die there."

"Would you mind coming out and showing me the spot? I'll pay you for your time."

"Oh, no, I wouldn't take your money, even if I could take you out there. But I can't do that. I know I sound like a coward, but I'm afraid to go out there. Lloyd should've fixed the fence after the cattle died, but he didn't. Instead he tried to chop down the big old oak that the statue's under. And that's when he died. I've never liked that part of the woods in all the years I've worked there, but I think Lloyd woke something up when he cut into the old tree, and I think that's how he died. Honest to God. The vet couldn't explain why the cattle died, and the doc couldn't say what killed Lloyd. But you ask me, it was something evil out there that done it."

With some prodding, Sam gave me directions that were simple enough that I could follow them on my own: walk northward into the woods until I reached a stream, follow it to its source, then continue in the same general direction until I reached the dark area. When I asked him how I would know when I was in the right place, he'd just told me, "Oh, you'll know for sure. The woods there are different. You can't miss the big oak once you're there, and the statue's right in front of it. But take my advice—think twice before you take a hike out there."

* * *

I was busy with all sorts of tasks around the property for the next couple of days, so I had difficulty finding time to take a jaunt into the forest. The sense of intrigue I had felt after talking to Sam began to fade, until the notion of some supernatural power lurking in the woods began to seem increasingly silly. I was slowly working my way towards deciding not to investigate it at all.

On the third night after my conversation with Sam, however, my mind was changed for me. Something startled me awake from a very deep sleep. What exactly woke me is hard to describe. I suddenly just had this strong sense that there was someone else in the room watching me as I slept.

I popped my eyes open and swiveled them around the room, careful not to move. It was pretty dark, but a few beams of moonlight shone in through gaps in the blinds, giving enough light for me to make out most of the room. As my gaze fell on the doorway, a huge shot of adrenaline surged into my system. The bedroom door, which I had closed and locked before going to sleep, stood open, and in the doorway stood a black figure. I couldn't make out much detail, but it looked like an adult man. Its eyes seemed to glow a faint green. I couldn't make out much else.

My right hand began moving towards the nightstand, where my revolver waited. I forced myself to move as slowly as possible so as not to betray movement to intruder.

When my fingers finally found the gun's grip, I moved fast—yanked up the gun with one hand, clicked on the lamp with the other, rolled out of bed and onto the wood floor. The revolver's sights came up as if by their own accord, in a straight line between my eyes and the doorway where the dark figure stood.

Only it wasn't there anymore. The doorway was empty. At first, I thought it might have just been a dream or my imagination. But that didn't last long, because I knew with absolute certainty that I had closed and locked the door before going to sleep, and now it stood wide open.

I felt under the bed for my flashlight. When I found it, I clicked off the lamp and waited a few minutes for my eyes to regain some of their night vision. Then I set about searching the house. I proceeded slowly and methodically, minimizing my usage of the flashlight, my gun always at the ready. I didn't find anyone, but I did discover that the front door of the house was unlocked. Again, I had a distinct memory of having locked it before going to bed.

When I looked more closely around the house, I found something else—footprints. They had been made by bare feet. I had missed them on the first pass through the house because they were faint, made of the same sandy soil that covered most of the ranch. They led all around the house—including the doorway to the bedroom I was using—and then out to the front porch. From there, they led down to the dirt driveway, then off towards the woods, where I lost them in the scrubby grass.

At this time of night, even the open and normally benign-looking pine and palmetto scrub near the house looked evil. I swept my light around a little, but saw nothing unusual. Though an adventurous part of me wanted to set off in pursuit of whoever was stalking me, another more prudent part made me stay put, at least until it was light again.

Naturally, I didn't get back to sleep that night—I just sat on a chair near the front door, my revolver on my lap. When dawn came, I got dressed, including snake-proof boots. I holstered my revolver and attached it to my belt, stuffed a small pack with a few snacks, and filled a canteen with water. Last, I retrieved my uncle's Ruger Mini-14 carbine from the closet, loaded it, and slung it over my back.

I headed into the woods, seeking the stream Sam had told me about. It was a beautiful late morning—oppressively humid, of course, but still relatively cool. The woods were alive—squirrels hopped, birds flitted, lizards ran and jumped, and I even spotted a few snakes crawling about. I heard, but did not see, larger animals shuffling through the brush—probably deer and wild hogs.

All in all, it was a very pleasant hike. I began to have second thoughts about my plans to sell the land—maybe I had been wrong about Florida. Maybe Florida was actually a nice place to live if you stayed away from all the densely populated areas. Maybe this ranch was a good place for me to end up after all my wanderings.

I didn't know much about ranching, but I knew how to ride a horse, and I could learn whatever else I needed to know. I could probably get a loan for more cattle. And if my walk through the woods was any indication, this place was full of wildlife. Once I got to know the land well, I could offer guided hunts to supplement my income, too. First, though, I would have to figure out what the hell was going on around here.

I soon found the little stream and began following it. It was shallow and spring-fed, the water clear as gin. After a half-mile or so, I reached the stream's head. There I stopped to rest for a few minutes, sitting down on a fallen log and eating a granola bar. I washed it down with a few swigs from my canteen, then got back up and continued in the same direction further into the woods.

I soon reached the broken remnants of a fence, and found a gap in it to walk through. On the other side, the foliage changed abruptly from mostly pine trees and palmetto scrub to big, gnarled oaks and cypresses. I noticed something else, too. There was no wildlife in the area. The rest of the woods had been teeming. But now, there was nothing. No birds, no squirrels, no snakes. Not even mosquitoes. And the silence was smothering. The woods darkened dramatically, the canopy above getting thicker, allowing much less light to permeate. The air, though cooler, became even more dense and humid.

Before long, I reached the big, scary-looking oak Sam had talked about. I knew it right away when I saw it. It was larger than all the others, and even more gnarled. It had a palpable sense of menace around it. The statue was there, too. The Seminole looked noble and defiant, but also angry. He stood on a coquina pedestal, his head was tilted upward. He seemed to be waiting in vain for some light to break through the dark foliage above. It was made of some kind of metal that had oxidized to a greenish-black color.

So this was where Uncle Lloyd had died—right by this statue, under this tree. As I approached the statue, I felt an almost electric sensation that I could not explain. I found no inscription or marking of any kind that might give a clue as to its age or origin, so I began looking closely at the big oak. I didn't find any markings on it, either, though I did find the spot where Uncle Lloyd had begun cutting into the tree with a chainsaw. From the look of it, he hadn't cut very far into it before he had collapsed and died.

I walked a little ways away from the tree and the statue and sat down for another break, eating another granola bar, taking some more deep swigs from my canteen, trying to figure things out.

The cattle had all gone through the broken fence and ended up in this area. Then, somehow, they had all died. Uncle Lloyd then decided that whatever had killed them had something to do with the wicked-looking oak, so he'd taken a chainsaw to it. But he'd died before he got very far in that task.

Though I couldn't be certain, it seemed quite plausible that what had killed the cattle had also killed Lloyd. He'd died as the livestock had—with no discernable cause. It also seemed reasonable to hypothesize that whatever had killed the cattle and my uncle—which was linked to this spot—was also linked somehow to whoever had stalked me last night. The question was, what linked it all—the clearing, the oak, the deaths, and the stalker? Then it hit me: the statue.

A hint of motion in my peripheral vision caught my eye. I glanced over towards the tree. When I had entered the clearing, the statue had been looking up. Now it was staring straight at me. Its hands, empty before, now each held a machete.

I stood up slowly, eyes fixed on the statue. Its eyes lit up with a green light.

I started backing away, mostly keeping my eyes on the statue, but glancing over my shoulder occasionally to make sure I wasn't about to back into a tree. As I backed up, I unslung the Mini-14 and flicked off the safety. It had a round chambered and nineteen more in the magazine. I had no idea if it would do a damn bit of good.

I'd gone about a dozen yards when the statue stepped down off its pedestal. It walked a few steps, then broke into a run. My military training kicked in and I began shooting, rapid-fire. My aim was true—the bullets struck the head and chest, but it only seemed to slow him down a little. I dropped the Mini-14 and ran for it. I could hear the statue's footfalls crunching through dead leaves behind me. In the distance the brighter part of the woods beckoned, but it felt like I was on a treadmill, running myself to death with no forward progress. I pushed my legs as hard as I could. I dared not look back over my shoulder, not wanting to know when the inevitable would come.

But it never came. I made it over the fence and out of the darkness. The footsteps behind me abruptly ceased, perhaps afraid to venture into a more sunlit area. I finally looked behind me. Nothing was there. I doubled over, panting, for several minutes until I caught my breath. Then I began the walk back to the house. I never went back to retrieve the carbine.

The next day, I headed into town to get supplies, after which I began replacing the fence around the dark woods. The new one I built was much sturdier, to keep people and livestock out—not to keep the statue in, because I knew a fence wouldn't hold it—at least, not at night. But I believed that if I demonstrated that I intended to leave that area alone, the statue would leave me alone.

Time proved me right. I decided to stay on the ranch after all. I eventually got a new herd of cattle, and started offering hunting for deer, hogs, and turkeys.

I venture out to the fence once a month to make sure that it's in good shape, and I fix it right away on the rare occasions when it isn't. So far, I haven't had any more trouble, and I don't expect to, so long as I keep myself and my livestock away from the darkest part of the forest.

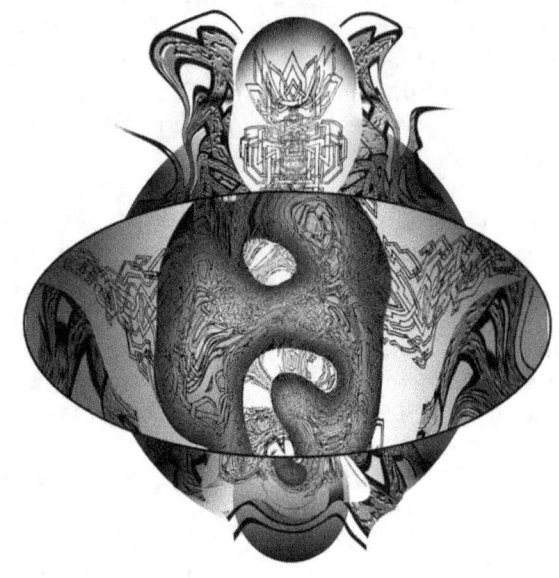

Lemon Wind

all day
nobody wanted
to talk

the sleeping bags
were still wet
from the storm
in Cholla Vista

Nothing went right.

But later the
wood we
burned had a sweet
unfamiliar smell

and all night
we could taste
lemons in the wind

— Lyn Lifshin

Early to Bed . . . . . Late to Rise

Across rubble and sand, a shrill wind blows.
No one knows what lies sleeping below.

Workmen jostle, shovel and shout,
Probing dark passages, hauling dirt out.

In a deep recessed chamber, dug beyond mortal recall,
A yellow eyelid flickers, linen dust falls.

Through debris and swirling dust, an encrusted door appears,
Sealed by priests of Amun Ra for three thousand silent years.

A chest begins to heave, bony joints stretch and bend.
A massive body rises, with sacred purpose to attend.

Lanterns flash upon the door, emblazoned with a glyphic script.
Eye of Horus, head of jackal, and perchance a curse to guard the crypt.

Trailing rotted cloth across the dusty floor,
A heavy figure lumbers toward the chamber door.

The seal is broken, the door pried open, and a wondrous scene unfolds.
Chariots, chests and bejeweled statues; everywhere, the glint of gold.

But while defiling eyes gaze upon the tomb,
A dark avenger suddenly looms.

Seized with fear, the desecraters scatter,
Save for one poor soul, whose skull is shattered.

Below rubble and sand, silence runs deep.
Once again . . . . . the mummy sleeps.

— Gary W. Davis

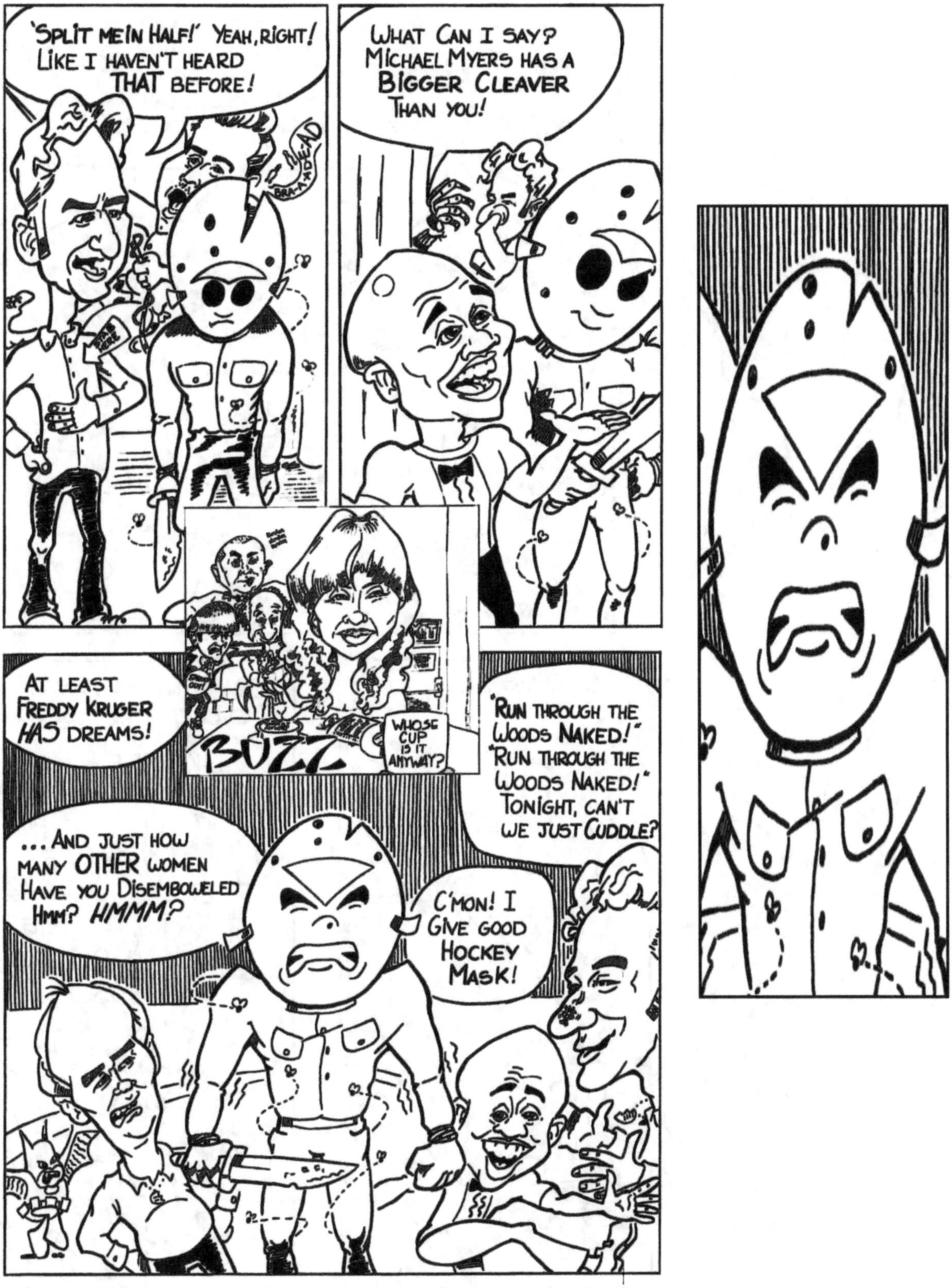

... and! Let's Go To Commercial

Ragtime: What Rough Beast

Story by T. Fox Dunham
Illustration by Paul Niemiec

"Why don't you stop playing kid-detective and get a real job, De La Fontaine." Krettle turned the dial on his iron pipe, set it to ersatz tobacco and sucked on the stem. Violet steam puffed from the bowl, smelled like wet cat. Bloody spider agents wouldn't leave me be. We'd be in the sorry house for war orphans together. He liked kicking me in the tick-tock.

"How about I come play storm troopers with you and your shadows? Sorry-Morry. I don't get my rocks off beating up old ladies."

He curled his thin lip above his teeth. Searchlights cut through the smoky night, glowing on infidel steam-fliers. Bombs whizzed down by the docks. I'd learned to turn off the rheostats to my ears, growing up with them—all denizens of the City of Lover's Be Lost did. "Watch that static," Krettle said. "Someone's going to cut a wax record on you. *Someone's* going to take an interest."

"Your Ministry ministers? Administer some true-thought on my head yarn? I'm just a cheap street-shoe—missing pets, cheating wives. I deliver misery to the people."

I spotted another one of the handmade sheets hanging on one of the gas poles burning—casting a sickness onto the broken streets of the Factory Quad in the city—the only city. Wasteland waited outside, always hungry beyond, the poisoned lands.

REWARD for ROUGH BEAST
Young'ons. See the workers of Rotfin
Steamworkers with gossip and talk.

One of Krettle's spiders pulled the poster off the pole, tore it to shreds and dropped the fragments into a street sewer. I'd shadowed for an hour and spied them defacing the signs, pouring petrol on my interest. Denizens vanished off the streets sans a song. A wet-faced momma hired me a week ago to find her son, and I linked the stories. I'd worn my shoes seeking and only heard rumors. People transformed into something beyond words. The family moved out of the flat without a word this morning, so no promised coin was coming to me. A body had to eat, and sometimes I had to pick through the rubbish for cases or I'd be digging in garbage for my tea.

"What's Rough Beast," asked a little spider. His boss sliced the agent's throat with a gaze.

"An old poem," I said, provoking them even more. "From the Before.

"Forbidden," Krettle said, adjusting his black bowler.

"A body named Yeats." Denizens whispered old poetry, the only thing to survive from that old time of glories—and of course drug, Ragtime.

Krettle took out his knife wheel—already wound up—and the knives of various and myriad blade sizes spun and sliced the air. He held it in the air between us. "I could nick you right now, me old boy, for that. It's on the forbidden list."

"But then you'd have to admit knowledge of it," I said and smirked. He grabbed the lapels on my imitation leather long coat, squeezed the elastic material then released.

"This is when you tell me to watch my bum?" I asked, playing out the full benefit of snapping his ass in a vice. He put away his spinning blade and beckoned his goons. They joined him, and his men merged into the mist, their footsteps drowned out by the toll of falling, detonating bombs that the bells in the old towers ringing. "I'll miss that sweet face!"

I joined the night, passing by late night workers off to their drone-stations at the factories. Many of them stumbled on malfunctioning limbs, dragging makeshift boilers and generators behind them on wheels. Grease pumped through tubes running from their clunky prosthetics. The Preacher's words scratched from the metal speakers hanging from the lamps and buildings. His words scratched over the amplifiers, gnawing at every air with tinny sounds and mutterings:

We will destroy the infidel across the sea!
We will smite him with our divine purpose.
Such is this life that does not belong to us.
Look not to the past, for it will deceive you.
This is the world of Ascension.

Colorful explosions decorated the ever-dark tide. Enemy steam-flies buzzed above my hair. Cannon fired from rooftop. I stomped through the slush back to my office in the Den Quad, stepping over junkies sleeping in the street. Portable metallic pumps pumped cheap Ragtime into their noses. The junkies cooed like children.

* * *

"You should let this one be," Tinker Fish said. Four work cycles passed, I found mechanic building clockwork toys in the alleys from the remains of tossed out mechanical limbs. He'd built a circus in an hour as I spied, sitting in the filth, building toys out of what had been people—more machine than flesh, more steam than blood. Fish spun about on three wheels in place of his limbs. He'd built a compact steam system powered by old food, bones, and reclaimed coal. His long beard tangled in his gears, and I freed him. "Bad energy this one. All smoky. Some truths are better not known. Understanding morphs you. That's how monsters be made."

"Have you noticed the office full of clients?" I said, sipping from ersatz coffee—tasted of old books and ink.

"It'll pick up, m'boy. Always does." His chair puffed away, and he spun to his workbench. I let him live in the cellar below my office, brought him food, fuel, new parts, and he built me things, did research, repaired my devices.

"When was dawn last declared?" I asked.

"Can't remember. At least several cycles ago."

I sipped my swill, wishing I had something to sharpen it. Fish read my mind and lifted up a flask then tipped it into my cracked tea cup. "Motor oil. Just brewed it. Mud in your eye."

I sipped it, and it burned out my eyes. "To Mary-Anne's furry bloomers!" I cheered, quoting something Fish always said.

"And the dumb-futz who married her. Oy. That would be me." He joined me in the toast and sipped back. "Oh. Got you something, my boy. I've repaired your pack."

I grinned like a child, and he handed me up the sleek metallic backpack. Metal framed it, and tin sheets shielded the clockwork. Compressed arms on screws attached along the side, released by buttons on a remote that attached to my belt. They delivered various tools to my hand, devices Fish added to aid me in my sleuthing. A silver hawk blazoned on the top, the symbol he'd given me.

"She's beautiful, Tinker." I rubbed his beard, and he blew it off then returned to his bench, fidgeting with a tinker truck. He built toys for one of the state orphanages and snuck them in, though the ministry staff would confiscate the toy if they found it. He probably had a plan for that too.

"Well if you're determined to do something incredible cork-brained, I might as well go with you on it," he said.

"We need the money, and it'll be a noticed case among the prols. They'll trust me after that. A creature of the night feeding on the poor, the disposed."

"Plenty of those. Call them *High Society*."

"It might just be the manifestation of the helplessness and fear felt by the workers. Old legends and street folk lore?"

He fiddled with the toy, turning its wheel. "Not just legends. Before I had my run in with an enemy steam-fly naught ten years back, I worked as a ministry excavator, digging up old city foundations to put in new flats. This city is built on another city that is built on another city. The sewers were streets once that had sewers that were streets. Tis' a maze buried under a maze and further." I nodded, sipping more of the bitter drink then spit out the oily flavor. "A paradise of tiny machines where humans flew among the stars and lived ever and ever sans illness and with song." An old sewer vent built above the work bench spewed bitter miasma into the cellar. I choked a bit and swallowed down bile.

"Stories always say that. Always the better realm."

"I saw it, below. The old world buried. The one that Preacher tells us is a sin to dream."

"Was it war?"

"No. Knowledge. The soul didn't come along with the brain. Ragtime."

"A drug for the wealthy, the bored," I said.

"It's said it creates monsters. Naturally. Beg pardon. The only thing to survive from the old world and found again—a disease waiting in an old oyster then eaten. It changes you. Some have various effects. You become … things. I saw it all. Rumor is the Ministry and Preacher use it to control the city— the opiate of the people—some old dude used to say in the old world. Marx … Groucho Marx."

I examined changes to the belt buttons attached to the pack. "What's this new button? It's blue."

"Read the inscription."

"ONLY IN CASE YOUR ASS IS DEAD. Shouldn't it be red?"

"Everyone else does red?" Fish said.

"What's it do?"

"Surprise. More dramatic that way.

I finished my drink and left Fish to his work. I had to hit the streets, go down to the factory and talk to the prols. And sometimes, Fish freaked me out with his stories. I daydreamed nightmares of the world beneath this world, buried and old, lost and shattered, haunting me beneath my thoughts— another world lost. Fish spoke of this city and its people—a race smarter and more beautiful than we, a people who built a paradise then lost to their natures, poisoned it, burned it to a land of ash. What hope had we?

* * *

So many sons and daughters of the City of Lovers Be Lost fought the Preacher's Holy War over the sea. None were ever seen again. Families hemorrhaged their best, their eldest, and few were spared, usually those who had been wounded by the bombs, to carry on the lineage.

The Preacher forbade names for the city. To name it was to give it power, and he would give no strength to the creations and devices of the terrestrial world; thus the denizens named the city in clandestine whispers, songs taken from an ancient poem that survived when passed on from the wretched survivors of the time Before.

I took to the streets during the bombing pause. Clouds strangled the night sky and would so for days, revealing no light or sun. I passed through the crowds of broken people, dragging their pumps, some of the workers more tubes and steam vessel than men. Street preachers cried out words of faith and propaganda from the tops of rubbish cans or balconies.

I approached the factory walls, waited until shift change and tried to slip in with the prols. I looked conspicuous, dressed in my brown leather coat and wearing a metallic pack on my back in queue with workers wearing gray overalls. Guards stopped me at the gate.

"What's your body doing here?"

"Selling vacuum cleaners," I said.

The line of workers passed by me, averting their eyes. Two thugs materialized at my back. I shouldn't have been so careless, always my problem.

"We know your body, De La Fontaine."

"Nice to know my press agent is earning his stew."

Their intercom honked, and the brute picked up and listened to another tube. He nodded a bunch like the screw joining his head to his fat neck had gone wonky. The guard gazed up at a window in the attached office building. A tall figure looked down on the street, playing and planning our lives like coal to burn.

"Lady Boss requires your body. Not here." He left the box, stepped out of the wall portal and led me along with two goons down the avenue, up the hillside. A single club survived, standing among rubble and bombed-out domiciles. I gagged on the stench of the rotting bodies entombed in the cement chunks. Scarlet letters flashed in pink mist along the outside of the single story place:

The Pink Gopher.

I'd heard of the watering hole but never stepped inside. The club grew like a root to a poison tree. All bad juju started at this toxic seed, and most of the stories I ended as a street seeker began in this moribund ship of fools.

"Go and wait for her in there. Buy her a drink. Let The Boss do what she likes with her foot."

"And you gorillas are going to linger out here?"

They shut their mugs, and I got the notion, so I gave them no commotion and carried myself in on forward motion. Pink shades project wild illusions, giving me delusions, from burning gas in jets along the walls. Line drawings, their shading and design hardly noticeable in the dim light, hung along the walls, depicting erotic scenes between all types of men and women. Pink fur lined the round tables.

"Hello my pet," said the Lady—renowned and infamous through the city. Poison Sumac extended her gloved hand. Her flat chest grew dark hair, bristling under her arms, and she wore a leather corset and blue panties, stockings and garters snapped tight. She made no effort to hide her manhood, bulging out from her knickers. Still her thin arms moved with elegance. She offered me her hand, and I kissed its back, close to the wrist. "And charming too. Seeker Fontaine."

"I didn't realize my body was this popular."

"You've handled many of my clients. I love to handle strange men."

"I'm meeting someone."

The Boss Lady's black business dress squeezed two sizes too small, as she slipped through the back entrance and sat down at a table close to the shallow stage. She beckoned me over—not entirely unattractive, a shock of white in her brunette hair and chiseled hands, feet in black heels. I sat at her table and sensed something cold and sticky on my seat. I had to lean forward because of my clockwork pack.

"I saw you knocking at my gate. I can only assume this is about my husband, Hermann?"

"Ja. Yes. Of course. Hermann." I didn't wish to reveal my intentions yet. I'd let her speak.

Poison Sumac strolled over, her garters snapping in her obvious and vulgar thigh bristles, carrying a cherry wood box. She set it on the table and pressed a catch in the heart of a male figure burned into the surface. The device unfolded like a puzzle box, releasing into sections that unfolded and released. I appreciated the symmetry. A small metal tank elevated and brass tubing emerged, completing the contraption.

"Do you need me to set this for you, my pet?" Sumac asked.

"I'm in fine fettle," the Boss Lady said. Sumac looked me over, grinned and softly growled. "My peepers peep it so." She slipped away. The Boss Lady took off her left shoe, emerged a foot missing most of its toes through holy black stockings then drove it right into my crotch. I lurched then calmed myself, a bit embarrassed about my behavior. I'd allow it, so she could be comfortable. The Boss Lady fed a small boiler with a clear liquid then from her purse removed a face plate—metal mouth, straps, and a tube which she plugged into the device. Ragtime. She removed a small vial of brown powder from the box and carefully filled a compartment on the side.

"I have an appetite for people. It only gets worse when I take Ragtime. It transforms you, depending on your nature. Quite powerful if you don't have self-control. You know what this is?" she asked.

"In all its glory and disease."

"Oh Seeker Fontaine. I didn't realize you were such a prude. That's … enticing."

"I won't flatter you, Madam. I can't stand to see the idle wealthy, sucking up the good pork and booze, breathing down your sick shit—and just using up what you can while you can before your workers rise up and rip it all down." The device whistled, and she showed me the faceplate. Barbs jutted from the inner face plate. It must have cut deep into the mouth when applied to the lips, securing the head so it couldn't be ripped away when the user lost their nerve. How appropriate. "So about your husband?"

"Ragtime changes people in different ways. He became … a monster." Something threw me: she just surrendered such private information with haste and without regard for her reputation. I'd keep an eye on that, note it for later. "I assume that's why you sniffed around my factory. You know, we have government contracts. We supply munitions for the Holy War."

"Most factories do now. Metal drawn from the mines and junkyards of the wasteland, converted, a bit of a kick added and then off to murder in a faraway land."

A phonograph played, set on a timer, singing some mournful woman I didn't understand.

"Where did he like to go to indulge his desires?" I asked. Everyone had a secret hole where they hid. She probably knew. Still, I felt like I missed something important here. All you can do is follow the clues.

"A pit in the factory—one of the old rooms from Before. But this is a lie. There was no Before."

The Boss Lady attached the mask to her mouth and strapped it in. She turned a dial on the alembic, and metal sang. Boiling steam flowed up the tube, and at first she screeched behind the mask, burned. And then she calmed, and her eyes floated, full of a spectral and wild light.

* * *

I returned to the office and my front window exploded, throwing me back into the street. I knew immediately the message and messenger. It took me a few minutes for my head to clear, led back to clarity by the metallic voice of the preacher yelling invective about the infidels over a loud speaker. My office burned, and some of the foundation collapsed.

"Fish!" I got to my feet, pressed a button on my belt, and a nozzle extended in my hand. I sprayed white foam from the tip as gears turned and my pack hummed, clearing a path through the heavy fire. I descended the stairs, dodging debris. The staircase collapsed behind me, and smoke wafted along the ceiling. I found Fish detached on his cot, and I picked him up.

"Fon'," he said coughing. "Grab the toy. The kids." I searched his bench and found the toy then stuck it in my pocket. We could get out through the old sewer vent; however I kept the ladder under the stairs. I couldn't jump the distance carrying the half-man Fish.

"Third button," he said. "New feature." I reached to my belt, pressed it, and a tethered harpoon released into my hand. I twirled the rope and grappled the grate, climbed, and we were through onto the street in moments, safely away from my office inferno.

I handed him the wind-up toy vehicle. "The nannies at the orphanage are going to find that pretty fast. You'll just break their little tick-tock hearts."

He shook his head, grinned then released a catch on the metal toy. Fish pressed it onto the pavement, and it flattened.

* * *

It had been a warning from the Preacher's Secret Police, though they'd probably meant for me to be inside when the building blew. Not like them to get the timing wrong. Death served as a germane warning, and it just vexed me. I would finish this now.

They knew everything. That was obvious. I'd know it soon too, and I knew that its magnitude could wreck the world.

The guards allowed me access to the cellar below the factory. The last shift toiled above, driving metal presses, stirring nitrate, building death to be delivered. I hadn't fought in the war, growing up in a state orphanage. Then I worked for like factory just like these drones, until I ran away, hit the streets and started doing favors, solving problems to survive.

The foundations of the factory didn't match the rest of the building—crumbling white concrete. The entire building should have collapsed, rotting away with the rest of the old city. Humans took to living in its warrens like rats, hiding away from the bombs. Rusting equipment, empty crates, barrels and rubbish filled the several storage rooms below the factories. Wheels turned in the ceiling, feeding onto the main floor. Pipes steamed. Boilers screamed. The workers dreamed.

Nothing obvious. Can't be found. I searched the walls and noticed dust and webs disturbed an empty work shelf. I ran my hand along the bottom of the shelf and found the release. The balanced furniture hung open on hinges, and I pressed a button on my belt. An arm extended. Clockwork ran. A portable flame ignited in my hands and cast away the shadows, reflected off a small disk. Fish was a bloody genius.

I'd found her husband's secret place, his private clubhouse, where he'd come to indulge his fantasies. He filled his appetites here. Sketches like those in The Pink Gopher lined the walls, though filled in color. I even found pornographic monochromatic plates and a lamp to emit them on the walls. I stepped through clothing littering the floor, and I examined the piles with my lamp: blood stained the worker's dresses and overalls. Some flesh remained, not much, and the odor hit me, gagging me.

"Go away!" a hollow voice yelled from the corner. A figure stood there at the edge of the light, and when I cast my lamp at him, he turned transpicuous—a spectral man made of moonlight.

"What are you?"

"I am no more, without substance. I cannot feel, eat, shag."

"You're a ghost?"

"Ragtime. I still dream of it, but I do not sleep. It is physical. I am ethereal. It transfigured me. I wasn't ready, took too much. I am trapped here now. She keeps me here with her mind. The bitch! I could never stand to her."

"Did you do this? Kill these people before you transformed?"

"No. The Rough Beast."

Slouches to Bethlehem to be born," I quoted. Then it struck me. I was in watery-willies now, quite the conundrum. My stomach twisted to collywobbles when I felt her pounce. I followed the husband's eyes and knew her vector, thus I dodged it. The Rough Beast hit the wall, spun around and roared. I recognized his mortal wife, the Boss Lady, from the toes missing on her foot—the limb she'd dug into my crotch. Her body elongated, stretched like taffy. Her naked body exaggerated, and much of her head flickered in and out of reality. Fur grew down her body, knotting around her legs. Her three mouths howled, and leather flesh bulged in hump on her back as she turned and clawed for me.

Ragtime presented myriad effects depending on your nature. By night, it transformed her into Rough Beast, and she must have turned back when the active chemical left her body. She possessed no self-control and sought to devour people—like most of the wealthy mucks. I paused and studied her eyes—looked physical. I pressed the familiar button on the belt and the nozzle slipped into my other hand. I sprayed the foam onto her face. It hardened fast, and she roared, throwing herself back into the wall.

"Now dear," said the ghost of Hermann. "You really must learn to control these urges."

"I'll give you two some privacy for marital bliss," I said and hauled my bum out of the secret room, racing for the stairs. She crashed through the wall behind me and screamed. The furniture splintered. I made it outside of the factory, joined by a throng of running workers. She burst through the building gates, peeled away the dried foam and gazed through me. She'd have my blood, and I knew I couldn't run fast enough. Well, what the hell? I reached to my belt and hit the big blue button:

ONLY IN CASE YOUR ASS IS DEAD

"I apologize if this is anti-climatic. I have it on faith that it's going to be amazing." I wasn't let down. Gears turned. Pipes popped out of the top of the pack. It unfolded on my back, shifting its weight outwards. Clockwork hummed. Wings expanded. At first, a small jet at the bottom fired a blue flame, shooting me into the dark sky. My boots melted, and I kicked forward, out of the range of the flame. Once I took airborne, the gears turned, motors churned, and the wings waved then flapped, keeping me ascended.

I laughed until my ribs ached, flying above the factory district of the City of Lovers Be Lost. "Kiss my flying, flapping … damn it." The Rough Beast unveiled its own wings behind me—that mass on her back—and flew like a bat, catching me fast. I dodged, and she clawed for me, her arms extending, turning to rubber. "That was anticlimactic. Still got to give the boy cheers."

I moved my shoulders, able to control my vector. The pack heated up on my back. It couldn't have much fuel—not designed for long flight. I had to find a place to land, where I could ditch the pack and perhaps hide among the burrows and homes. I knew the city well around my office, and I looked for the smoking ruin. Air raid sirens howled. Of course. Enemy steam-flies flew low onto the city. I could see them through the thin layer of the cloud ceiling. The ships looked remarkably like ours—rectangular, flying on wings, gears turning on the side.

I dodged a bomb. I hadn't done it on purpose, and I felt it fall by my body, hitting me with the air pressure. A building burst into flames, and heat surged my body, burning the hair off my arms. I dove through the falling gravity bombs, and one of them hit my left wing. It snapped clear off, and I wobbled in the air. Going down. I controlled my descent, allowing the Rough Beast to close any remaining distance. She clawed at my head, slashing my cheek. I tasted my own blood spraying in the cold winds. I dropped too fast, nearly hitting the flats by my flattened office. I hit the street, tumbled, and the pack tore off my back. She landed close behind me.

"Our souls will always be free," I informed the Rough Beast as she approached me, claws out, the bottom of her head phasing in and out of reality, half transferred to whatever ethereal plane that now imprisoned her husband. "I don't know why I said that. Seemed like cool last words." I limped back, nearly falling into the debris. Bullets ripped by my head. Krettle and a small division of soldiers open fire, waiting for us. I dove into my office debris, finding cover.

"Keep at it!" he yelled.

"Rough Beast!" I yelled out, but they couldn't hear me. Krettle must have been keeping eyes on my body and beheld our final flight through the city skies. They'd used me. Blowing up my shop had been for me to witness. I had to admire it a little. They had to hide the effect of Ragtime. The Ministry, our Preacher, controlled the city with it. The Rough Beast howled in obvious agony as they sawed her into pieces with their weapons. I knew they'd turn their weapons on me as a witness, so I dug my way to the hatch leading into the cellar, hoping to escape through the sewers again as we had when the place burned down.

If I survived, I'd bill them.

The Machine Planet

When the machines took over,
Defeated man to extinction,
They strip mined the surface flat,
Hollowed out the interior
In search of iron ore
And then began to build their own
Kind, constructed conception,
A manufactured reproduction
Until the entire planet was covered
With cog wheels and levers,
Intermittent gears and pistons,
And the great smoke stacks
Belched orange fire into
The coal black atmosphere
And nightly rose the prayer
Of the thankful machines:
A clang. A clang. A clang.

— K.S. Hardy

Join the Crew of the *Aristarchus* on an epic voyage of discovery in *The Solar Sea*

Humans settled the Moon and satellites orbiting the Earth were a common sight, but with the abolition of NASA, humans had no desire to go further and space exploration died.

Then, a technician from the Very Large Array, a radio telescope in New Mexico, discovers powerful particles orbiting Saturn's moon, Titan, which could be a new energy source. Strangely enough, following the discovery's announcement, whales around the Earth changed their songs overnight.

As scion of the powerful Quinn Corporation, Thomas Quinn builds a solar sail to find the source of these particles in Titan's orbit. He gathers the best and brightest team to pilot his craft: Jonathan Jefferson, an aging astronaut known as the last man on Mars; Natalie Freeman, a distinguished Navy captain; Myra Lee, a biologist specializing in whale communication; and John O'Connell, the technician who first discovered the particles. All together they make a grand tour of the solar system and discover not only wonders but dangers beyond their imagination.

Drawing on his experience as an astronomer, David Lee Summers has created a story that is both exciting and plausible, one that can be enjoyed by both the young and young-at-heart who enjoy looking at the planets on a clear night and dreaming of what could be.

"In *The Solar Sea*, David Lee Summers creates a page-turning yarn with some of the most dramatic characters I've read in years. You won't want to put it down, and when you're done, you'll only want more."
— J Alan Erwine, author of *The Opium of the People*.

". . . I thought that the book was very good. It had an easy to follow plot that even those who've never read science fiction could follow. I would recommend this book to anyone who enjoys a good read."
— MSwan, Nebraska, USA - Flamingnet Reviews

Available at Amazon.com, BN.com, and Hadrosaur.com
Learn more at TheSolarSea.com

George Lucas's Lost Flying Saucer
or: How I Traveled Somewhere in the Galaxy Without Even Trying

Story by Richard P. Nixon
Illustration by Kathy Ferrell

I WANT TO BELIEVE

February 12, 2

Flying saucers don't exist, right? Wrong! I know because I found one.

I was thirteen years old. I no longer played with some of my favorite toys, my first pimples had just begun to bloom, girls weren't icky anymore, and I knew what I wanted to do in life; make movies. My best friend Chuck and I had fancied ourselves as filmmakers forever, it seemed, but as our skills had evolved so, too, had our challenges. We realized we needed help. Our friend Toby joined in about a year ago, and he proved to be as loyal and reliable as they come. Why, he even sprained an ankle falling out of a tree saving our main camera. I still feel kinda bad for him but, fortunately, he hardly limps anymore.

Anyway, we had our eye on entering an amateur film making contest with the top prize of an all-expenses paid week-long internship at a real movie studio working with a big time director, and there were rumors that even George Lucas himself might be on hand. I just knew we were going to win; we were going to see wizards make magic. All we had to do was come up with one reasonably realistic-looking flying saucer.

Dad suggested the local university's theatrical department. "I know the director there, Mr. Franklin," he said. "He's an old friend. I'll give him a call."

A few days later Toby, Chuck and I hiked up to the university. Mr. Franklin was very nice, telling us how he knew Dad from his work at NASA training the astronauts. "Those were good days," he said. "And you've grown into a fine young man." He told us that he wasn't sure if there was anything useful in the storage yard but that we could look around as much as we wanted. "Just be real careful, and don't get lost," he added with a smile.

We made our way to the yard, and when we opened the gate it was as if we'd stepped into the Promised Land. The place was huge!

"Where do we start?" Toby said.

"I don't know," I replied. "Maybe we should split up?"

"Looks like there's everything here," Toby said.

Chuck nodded. "Yeah. Maybe we'll get lucky," he said, "And find the spaceship someone ripped off from that Lucas movie a couple of years ago."

Toby and I groaned. "Uh huh," I said. "That was like five hundred miles from here."

Toby ran ahead saying, "I'll start over here. I mean we have some idea what to look for. How hard could it be?"

Nearly three hours later we were sweaty and dirty and pretty much spent but still hadn't found anything remotely resembling a spaceship. I paused to take a deep breath, thinking maybe Mr. Franklin knew the storage yard better than we imagined. I was about to pack it in when I spotted an old canvas tarp under boxes and props that looked to me like someone had hastily piled up in a clumsy attempt to hide something. "Hey guys! Over here! Give me a hand!" I said.

We dug down and cleared away the clutter. I pulled away the tarp revealing a large and shiny gray metallic object underneath. "Are you kidding me?" I said.

"That's a flying saucer," Chuck said.

"Gosh, that's big," Toby said.

I nodded. Roughly larger than a couple of minivans and flared around the middle, the saucer could have come from any number of science fiction movies from the fifties. I moved closer for a better look. There wasn't a lick of gaffer tape or wire or even a place to secure a rope. My heart began pounding. I looked at Chuck nervously—this was almost too good to be true. "What do you think?"

Chuck smiled. "We need a truck."

"And a crane," Toby said. "There's just no way we can move it. It's too big."

"Hmm," I said. "Let's get some more stuff out of the way before we decide it's hopeless. Okay?" I didn't have any idea how we were going to move the saucer but knew we had to figure it out. After all, no way could we set up for shooting in the storage yard. I put my hands on the spaceship as if it would somehow tell me what to do. It felt cold and slippery, like nothing I'd ever felt before. It made my fingers tingle and my hair rise as if charged with static electricity. "Whoa…" I said.

Toby touched it too, and instantly pulled back as if shocked. But he reached for it once more and ran his hand over its surface. "That's unreal," he said.

I was beginning to think the same thing. It's just a prop, I reminded myself wondering just how many millions of dollars it had cost to make. I don't know what made me do it, but I gave the spaceship a little shove as if hoping it weighed much less than it looked. It moved. Not much; maybe an inch but that wasn't the point. It had moved, and I didn't even push that hard. "Hey guys," I said. "Look at this." I shoved the spaceship again, and it moved again.

"What the heck?" Toby said.

Chuck's mouth gaped.

"Help me," I said.

We all pushed but were able to move the saucer only about a foot before it just stopped despite our efforts. "That makes no sense," I said.

Toby, walking around to one side of the spaceship, suddenly lit up. "It's stuck."

"Really, genius?" Chuck said.

"No, I mean it's stuck because something's in the way."

The spaceship had gotten hung up on a pipe sticking out of the ground. "We could try lifting it," I said.

"Are you kidding?" Chuck said. "The thing's got to weigh a ton."

"Yeah, and we were able to move it. Your point?" I said.

Somehow we managed to get a good enough grip to get the saucer over the pipe, and once free, it glided with little effort except when scraping over imperfections in the floor. I racked my brain trying to come up with a plausible explanation but the only thing that came to mind was that this was no ordinary movie prop. I'd seen enough of the behind-the-scenes bonus features to know most models and props were slapped together with duct tape and chewing gum and relied on cables and pulleys and electric motors and such to work, and always with someone operating the controls. What we had was something else, something extraordinary. "You know what?" I said trying hard to contain my excitement. "Suppose this isn't a movie prop at all?"

Chuck and Toby shot me puzzled looks.

"This is more like something Lucas would have his effects wizards put together so he could drive it around his ranch for his own amusement."

Toby grinned. "That would explain a lot."

Chuck disagreed, shaking his head. "Then how did it end up here?"

How indeed? I thought.

"I bet it's military!" Toby said. "It probably got sold at a surplus auction by mistake. I heard about this guy who bought a missile guidance system for a few dollars and brought it to pawn shop trying to score some quick cash."

I'd heard of that sort of thing happening, too, but there were no markings or anything like that to indicate it being military. "Na," I said. "I think this belonged to Lucas."

We draped the tarp back over our saucer and told Mr. Franklin that we'd found something we could use but needed to get it out through the back gate. He smiled and called a security guard to help

us. Thankfully, he didn't question what we were moving or how.

It took nearly an hour to get the saucer back to our fort. Okay, so it wasn't so much a fort as it was the nerve center of our production operation. I chuckle each time I think of it that way, but it was a pretty accurate description. We had double-glazed windows and skylights, insulated walls, proper doors and most important of all, electricity. Not just a few battery-operated lanterns but real mains power from a bank of salvaged solar panels and deep-cycle batteries feeding a grid-compatible inverter. If we'd scrounged enough wire, we could have made some pocket money selling the excess back to the power company had we wanted. We had everything we needed in our fort; overstuffed chairs, a refrigerator, small air conditioner, game console, computer; even high-speed Internet access.

"How are we going to secure the saucer?" Toby said. "I mean, the way it moves, one gust and it'll be gone."

We tried crisscrossing the saucer with ropes tied to tent stakes we'd hammered into the ground, but the ropes just slipped off. So we used gaffer tape instead—that did the trick.

"So now what?" Chuck said.

"So now we look for the way in," I said. I began sliding my hands over the saucer's skin, feeling for any imperfection that might be a button or latch. I had worked my way about half way around when all of a sudden symbols glowed light blue under where my hands passed over. "Hey guys," I said. I repeated the hand movement, and the same symbols glowed again. "Check this out!"

"Whoa…" Chuck said.

"Those look like Imperial symbols from the movies. Probably means, 'Press Here'," Toby said.

Chuck clipped Toby on the arm. "I suppose you speak Bochi, too."

"Noooo." Toby recoiled. "But Lucas was always doing that sort of thing. Remember Club Obi Wan in Indiana Jones and the Temple of Doom?"

I pressed on the symbols. There was a click and then a low hum and suddenly an oval outline larger than a man appeared in the same light blue glow as the symbols. In moments, the material inside the outline disappeared. "I found the hatch!" I knew Lucas was into some very cool stuff, but this … this was way cool, even for him.

"Gotta be military." Toby said.

I nudged Toby and said, "Stick your head inside."

All too eager to please, Toby smiled and stepped toward the opening.

Chuck shot me a dirty look.

I sighed and rolled my eyes. "Hold up, I'll do it," I said, pulling Toby out of the way. I shone my tiny blue-LED key ring flash-light into the craft. The inside looked like it was made of the same slippery metallic material as the skin. The chamber lit up when I eased my hand inside. "Much better," I said under my breath. My heart pounded and my mouth went dry, and I was scared but I had to keep going, had to find out what this thing really was. "This could be some kind of an airlock."

"Why would there be an airlock?" Toby said. "Unless…"

"Come on, Toby. It's supposed to be a space-ship, right?" Chuck said. "So of course they would have that to make it look right on screen. Duhhh…"

"I thought we thought this was some kind of cool machine Lucas used to fly around his ranch." Toby quipped.

"Well it could be both, you know," I said.

"Do you think we should get your dad?" Chuck said.

"Why?" I shot back. I could think of a hundred reasons why but didn't offer any of them. I bit my lip and ran my hand along the walls hoping to find the controls to open an inner hatch. Sure enough more glowing symbols appeared on the wall, and when I pressed on them, another oval outline appeared before the material within it dissolved with an abrupt hiss as if I'd just opened a can of soda. I poked my head inside.

"What do you see?" Chuck said.

Despite its rather compact dimensions, the second interior chamber was surprisingly roomy. "There's a single seat flanked by oval control panels perched facing a flat dimpled console, and not much else." I said.

"Only one seat?" Toby said.

I chuckled. "I suppose if you're Mr. Lucas, one's all you need."

Chuck leaned in behind me and said, "So what do you think?"

"I think I'm dreaming." That's when I spotted a large manila envelope wedged between the seat and the left control panel. "Hold on a minute, I've found something else." I nearly fainted when I saw "Top Secret" and "Property of United States Government" emblazoned in bold red on the front. "You guys are not going to believe this!"

Chuck had a very serious look on his face as he rifled through the contents.

Toby was more direct. "Told you so."

I did my best to hide my concern. "Come on, guys," I said. "This is just part of the prop." But as I flipped through page after page I couldn't help but think about how real they looked. They all were marked "Top Secret" and had numbers and lots of technical words on them. A couple were even signed and had official looking stamps. *Na*, I thought. We found the saucer in a storage yard. If it were military it sure wouldn't have been in a place like that, right?

* * *

Through trial and error we figured out how to turn on various colored lights and alien-looking readouts, and were ready to start shooting. I played The Space Explorer, and there were moments sitting in that pilot's seat waiting for the cameras to roll that I could shut out the others and imagine myself flying to the far reaches of the universe. Chuck shouting, "Action!" always brought me crashing back to Earth and reality. I needed to come back when I could be sure of being alone.

My alarm went off right on time at 12:30 AM. I got dressed, grabbed my flashlight, and headed for the fort. I got the lights and cameras and computer equipment running, sat down in the pilot's seat and began going through the motions of working the controls as if I were on some interstellar mission. "This is Commander Taggart to Earth control," I said. "All systems go. Awaiting take-off clearance." Everything went great until the blinding flash and…

* * *

"I don't remember how I got to the hospital, Dad," I said.

Dad nodded.

"But that's not all."

"Oh?" Dad said, leaning in closer, his face creased with worry.

"Yeah. I…"

A sharp knock on the door cut me off, and before Dad could say anything, two men in black suits came in.

As Dad got up, the first man flashed a badge. "My name is Agent Smith. This is my partner, Agent Jones, and we'd like to ask a few questions."

My heart began to pound, my breathing became rapid and shallow, and my stomach felt like it does when you feel like you're falling. "Is this about the flying saucer?" I blurted.

Agent Smith looked puzzled and narrowed on

me. "Flying what?"

I began trembling. I swallowed hard and drew in a huge breath. "The flying saucer? We were making a sci-fi movie and found a flying saucer prop only it turned out to be real. I know 'cause after the flash of light the whole thing took off and on the front view screen I could see the Earth, the Moon, and an ocean of stars like I never imagined before. The ocean of stars turned to a kind of glowing blur and an instant later I was in orbit around another planet, green I think. It was just like Earth in so many ways yet completely different," I gushed in one breath.

Agent Smith grinned. "What an imagination," he said, shaking his head. "Flying saucers! Space travel! Alien planets!" He chuckled. "Son. You've been watching too much television. The FBI doesn't investigate flying saucers."

"Anymore," Jones added.

Dad said, "My son is very tired."

"Uh huh, uh huh. I understand. This won't take but a minute or two," Smith said. "Was it you who brought your son to the hospital?"

Dad shook his head. "No."

"Hmm…" Smith said. "Reception said that you did."

"I can't explain," Dad said.

Smith glanced at his partner. "I see."

"A man brought my son into the ER, said he was unconscious, and next thing they knew the guy was gone."

"And you've no idea who this person was?" Jones said.

"No."

I shook my head when Smith looked at me. "Any idea where he might be now?" he said.

"Of course not. I didn't know anything had happened," Dad said. "My son woke up, told them who he was and, well, here we are. All the doctors can tell me is that he's registering an unusually high electrical field."

"Residual effect of being struck by lightning," Smith said.

"Lightning?"

The agents nodded looked at each other and nodded. "After surveying the scene and looking at the evidence," Jones said, "We have determined that's what happened."

"That," Smith added, "Would also account for your son's imaginative story."

"Really?" Dad tensed.

"Oh yes," Jones said. "Definitely."

"But there isn't a mark on him," Dad protested.

"It was an indirect strike," Jones said.

Smith nodded.

Before Dad could question either of them further, Smith said, "Thank you. We're done here, for now." He handed Dad a business card he retrieved from his wallet. "If you think of anything to add, call." He grinned again.

Dad was not amused. "Now look here—who is this mysterious person? Why are you looking for him, and if he's running from the FBI, why did he risk bringing my son here?"

Smith shook his head slowly. "I've no idea." He motioned to his partner who opened the hospital room door. "But if you see him again, or anyone you think might be him, call us." The agents left.

After a few moments, Dad looked at the card and said. "That was very strange."

"It wasn't a lightning strike," I said quietly. "Dad? I don't trust them."

Dad chuckled. "You seem to have inherited your mother's judgment of character."

I swallowed hard. "I miss her," I said.

"I know son. I do too."

It seemed like the longest silence passed between us before I said, "Dad, I'm scared."

Dad gave me a hug. "Don't worry, son. Everything will be okay."

* * *

The hospital released me the next day, saying they had no real explanation as to what might have happened to me. As I got in the car to go home, I spotted Smith and Jones parked across the parking lot. "Dad," I said, pointing toward the men as covertly as I could.

Dad nodded gently. "I know," he said.

Smith and Jones followed us home, and parked down the street. I figured they expected the mystery man to show up again, but I didn't have time to dwell on it as Toby and Chuck came barreling up on their bicycles just as I got out of the car.

"How are you?" said Chuck.

"Yeah!" Toby said. "We heard you got struck by lightning!"

I grinned. "You aren't going to believe the story I've got."

"Now, hold on a minute," Dad said. "Before you guys get too involved in catching up, Derek's very tired and needs his rest."

"Aw, Dad" I complained. "I feel fine. Besides, the doctors said there was nothing wrong with me."

Dad smiled. "Even still, take it easy, okay?"

Us three boys nodded innocently and waited for Dad to go in the house.

"So what's this story you've got for us," Chuck said.

I glanced down the street to the FBI men. "Shhh," I said, "Not here." I started walking toward the fort. "How's the saucer?"

Chuck shook his head. "The saucer's gone, and so's a bunch of our stuff."

"What?" I said.

"Yeah," Toby added.

I took off in a sprint, with Chuck and Toby following close behind. When we reached the fort the saucer was right where it was supposed to be.

"What the…?" Chuck said. "I swear it was gone."

"Yeah," Toby said. "No way was it here yesterday. No way!"

Inside the fort looked like someone had been searching for something in a hurry. There were papers on the floor, and stuff taken out of drawers and just strewn about.

"They even raided the fridge!" Toby said, pointing to the open door on the now-empty fridge.

Unfortunately, both the cameras and the computer were still gone. "I bet it was the FBI guys," I said.

"FBI guys?" Toby said.

"Yeah. There's a couple of them waiting in a car near the house. That's why I couldn't say anything."

"What do they want?" Chuck said.

"They asked me about the guy who dropped me off in the emergency room. Said he looked just like my dad."

"Wow." Toby said.

I told them the rest of my story as I walked toward the saucer. I wanted to check it out to see if it was okay inside. The craft's hatch suddenly opened. A familiar figure popped his head out. "Dad?" I said, confused.

Dad turned to me.

"How did you get here?" I said. "I thought you were back at the house."

Before he could answer, a bolt of energy exploded against the saucer. Dad wobbled, stunned.

"What the?"

"They've come for me," Dad said, hunched over. "Go! GO!"

A snap to my left caught my attention. Smith and Jones were about twenty yards away. Smith fell to one knee and took aim with some kind of ray gun

pulsing red at the tip.

I lunged toward the saucer, frantically waving my arms and yelling "No!" I don't know why. Maybe I was being stupid, but at the time all I could think about was protecting Dad. Just as Smith fired, however, someone came out of nowhere and tackled me. I hit the ground hard with the wind knocked out of me. As I lay gasping, the energy bolt exploded nearby. I screamed, "DAD!"

It was suddenly quiet except for the ringing in my ears and me sobbing and repeating, "Dad." I probably wouldn't have noticed the vibration that tickled the small of my back or the warm rush of air had I not suddenly been engulfed in the intense white light. Not the harsh, blinding flash of another energy bolt exploding; this was more like a comforting blanket. That may sound odd, and maybe it is, but I was no longer thinking about danger.

"Wh-what happened?"

My heart jumped. "Dad?" I scrambled over and threw my arms around him. "I thought…"

Dad squeezed me tight. "It's okay."

Fear suddenly gripped me. "The agents!" I whipped my head from side to side looking for Smith and Jones.

"They're gone," Chuck said flatly. "So's the saucer."

"Wait … what…," Toby was talking and hyperventilating at the same time. "I-I don't understand," he said. "Y-your dad was in the saucer at the same time he was tackling you to the ground?" Toby's breathing slowed. "How can that be?"

I looked at Toby. "That wasn't my dad."

As for our epic film, well, I like to think there's a bright side to everything. Sure we had lost our cameras and computer, but it turned out that all the footage had been automatically mirrored on a cloud drive. Mr. Franklin gave us a couple of really excellent second-hand hi-def cameras and a computer so powerful that we had to upgrade our solar panel array to handle the extra load, so with some new footage edited in with the old we were able to produce something quite impressive. Unfortunately it all came together after the competition deadline, but we sent it in anyway with the idea that you just never know. For our effort we each received an autographed photo of Mr. Lucas in front of our flying saucer and a personalized letter that read simply, "The secret to film is that it's an illusion. George."

We're looking forward to making our next movie, having discovered Toby's uncanny knack for creating spaceships and alien worlds and just about anything we can imagine on the computer. We still talk about what happened, but I doubt we'll ever know. Not for sure, at least. My friends and I tried to figure things out, and we came up with all kinds of explanations almost as fantastic as what we actually experienced. In the end, though, no one wanted to ask the one question I knew we were all thinking: would they ever come back?

First Contact

Billy-Bob chased the last bit of gravy around his plate with a morsel of biscuit before popping it into his mouth and wiping his fingers on his overalls. He nodded across the table to his cousin Ray.

"So whatdidja do wit that saucer gizmo they come in?"

"It's up on blocks out behind the barn. I already sold a lot of it off to da scrap yard. They pay good money fer stuff made of 'luminim. You know, beer cans n' shit like that."

Ray nodded, then called out in the direction of the kitchen of the double-wide, "Hey, Sis! What's takin' so long wid that pie?" He looked back at Billy. "Dat wife of yours shore can cook, lemme tell you."

"Yep," agreed Ray scooping up the last morsel on his plate with a fork. "Tastes just like chicken. But don't let on ta none o' them city folk or they'll be sendin' the game warden around again, jes' like they did with them other 'en-dane-gered' species."

"Ain't that a fact," agreed Billy. "I don't care what anybody sez, them little gray fellers is some mighty good eatin'."

— M.E. Brines

Speaking Cicada

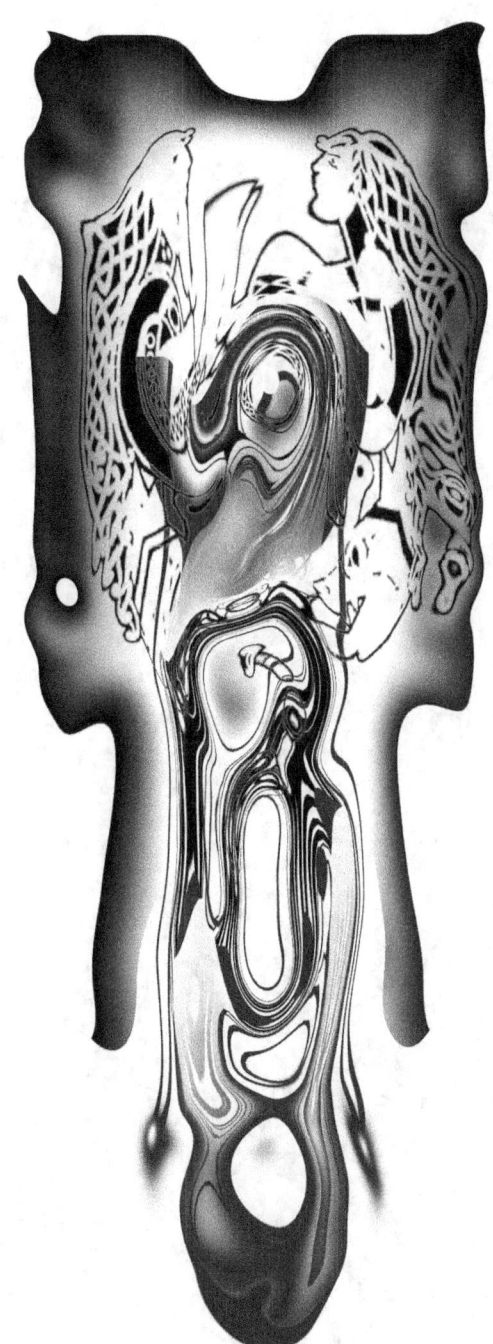

The cicadas are driving me crazy.
Their constant buzzing echoes inside my skull
like a cosmic jackhammer.
Still I am compelled to climb a tall tree
in the effort to capture a cicada alive.
My son, my beautiful infant son
is slow to speak his first words,
much later than other children.
My wife is so worried
that I try to reassure her,
"He looks so happy."
The matter is decided by the boy's grandmother,
my mother,
who announces that it is my paternal responsibility
to climb a tall tree filled with buzzing insects
and kidnap a cicada.
It is an old Mexican custom
when a child is slow to speak
a buzzing cicada
is held to the silent child's tongue.

Cicada's are such hideously ugly bugs,
looking like a cross between grasshoppers and beetles
with big square heads holding great big googly eyes.
As I hold the rabidly buzzing insect
in front of the face of my infant son
his eyes fill with both disgust and wonder.
He looks so curious, happy and innocent
that I cannot bring myself
to perform this act of brujo voodoo
but before I can pull the bug away
My baby boy lunges forward
and chomps off the cicada's head
as if it were a chocolate bar.
He chews, smiles, and says his first words.
His first words form a question.
"Why is the sky blue?"
which is quickly followed by another question
and then another.
Why Why Why Why
but he never bothers to ask the most important question.
My quickly growing baby boy never inquires
why the cicadas are driving me crazy.

— Gary Every

Demons of Disease

Story by Abra Staffin-Wiebe
Illustration by Laura Givens

Dr. H. Iyaci fumbled a packet of wipes out of his pocket and cleaned his hands. He knew better than most laymen how swift the spread of Disease could be. There had been a sick woman shopping in the grocery store, scattering the seeds of disease in her wake. What if she had something you could die from?

Most people didn't think twice about visiting the places where they courted Death: a crowded subway car, a public restroom, or a mall with recirculated air.

Dr. Iyaci knew only two other people who recognized the danger, Dr. Maria Injack and Dr. Wilfred Shunn. They were brave people, who had spent their whole lives struggling against Death and its handmaiden Disease. They had made so many sacrifices they were practically saints. He would aid their cause considerably tonight by sharing with them the results of his latest study.

Viruses were tricky things, the helper demons of Disease and Death, changing constantly so one could never quite pin them down, but he had finally figured out their secret. Now he could create a weapon against them.

While Dr. Iyaci waited to cross the street, a bum sidled up next to him, muttering a plea for a few bucks. As he recoiled, the vagrant broke into a hacking cough. Dr. Iyaci fled into the street.

He heard the screech of brakes too late to do more than turn and face the headlights rushing his way. Then he was flying through the air. He felt the impact when he hit the ground, but there was no pain. No pain. Bad sign, he thought. He tried to move, but the most he could do was paw weakly at his shirt pocket, where he kept his wallet and the all-important Cryogenics, Inc. card.

* * *

Two hundred years later….

Reict listened half-heartedly to the sermon. He believed the doctrine, but he'd heard it all before.

"…and let us not be caught sleeping by evil Death, and his minion Disease. Let us put our faith in the Holy Injection of the Spirit…."

Reict leaned forward to watch the ritual. He had read the grimoires of the holy doctor-priests, before he had been expelled from their numbers for heresy. He understood what he watched, unlike the rest of the congregation.

The priest made the Sign of the Needle, lifting his hand to his arm and pushing the thumb in. The congregation followed the gesture. Then the priest put out his hand, and an acolyte reverently laid the syringe containing the Holy Injection on it. Reict knew what was actually in the syringe—a virus containing gene splices of different diseases to trigger an immune reaction in the body of the child. It would keep the child safe from those demons of Disease that the priests could battle. After inoculating the child and introducing him to the congregation, the priest moved on to the announcements.

"As is the will of the All-Curer, John Currin has become a Holy Martyr," the priest said. "Remember, if thine eye offends thee, pluck it out. If thy body is infested with the minions of Disease, destroy it. Then thy healthy soul may arise to join the Heavenly Healthy in Paradise, where there is no Disease and no Death."

Reict looked at the plaques of the Martyrs imbedded in the walls of the church. His gaze wandered across the Church as the rest of the congregation bent their heads in prayer. It was a beautiful building. Light poured in through the stained glass windows of the Saints. Closest were St. Edward Jenner, warding off the demon Smallpox with the light of Holy Purity, and St. Pasteur, fighting off a vicious slavering dog possessed by the demon Rabies. The Holy Church had eliminated all such animals, easily possessed by Disease. Sometimes Reict wondered what it might have been like had a few healthy specimens been allowed to live. It was a sinful thought, inspired by Death. At the front of the church, two windows showed the Holy Founders of the Faith, St. Injack and St. Shunn. They were clothed in the purest white, with surgical masks over their faces and halos shining above them.

Reict grimaced internally. The Church did not acknowledge St. Iyaci, the Holiest of them all. Those of the True Faith, however, strove to re-create the work that Death had destroyed. The church declared them heretics, to be stoned on discovery, not even allowed the dignity of martyrs.

After the sermon, Reict rose and filed out of the church. A ten-minute walk away, he turned down an alley and rapped on a door.

"Operation?" a whispered voice queried.

"Defrost," Reict said, scanning the surroundings for anything that might be a threat.

When the door swung open, he slipped inside

"What progress?" he asked the gathered believers.

"Once I get back the tissue sample results, I will know which revival solution to use," a woman told him. "The Holy Saint will rise and walk amongst us once more."

They heard a knock on the door. Her eyes brightened. "That's probably the messenger with the results."

The instant the messenger was admitted, she snatched the printout from his hands and began skimming it. All color fled her face.

"He is infected. The demon Flu has him in its grip. If we revive him, the demon will walk among us," she whispered. "What should we do?"

Reict did not hesitate. "As one of the Founders, he had the greater holy strength to know what must be done. Cremate the body, lest contagion wakes and the demon spreads. It is as he would have wished."

He turned away. Much knowledge would die with St. Iyaci, but the True Faith would re-create his work. When their time came, they would honor him as a martyr.

Post-Funeral Mission (to Mars)

As the airplane enters the towering clouds, Billy spies wispy ghosts and shifting white valleys. What is turbulence to everyone else, to Billy is scratching fog-fingers and monstrous tongues.

His grandma snores beside him. Others resign to airport novels, electronics, and the anticipation of the cart. Humming engines and whooshing air vents backdrop the cries of a baby, of two teenage girls absorbed in gossip.

Billy peers out the cold, turbid window, sees Harryhausen beasts run amok through the floating landscape: dinosaurs gnawing on cars and bridges, a distant Cyclops ripping a train off its tracks.

A break in the clouds reveals a stretch of suburbia, baseball fields where an interest in sports fell short of home plate. All around, long thin roads blink with ant-cars: "More people die in car crashes than in planes, you know," his parents once said, not long before the accident.

The edge of an approaching cirrus cloud swirls over the wings: here comes Conan through the smoke of battle, sword dripping with ruddy sunlight. He charges an army of angry skeletons—bones and skulls sailing through the fog.

Suburbia slides back into view, its rooftops the color of cigarette ash, a string of retention ponds like chicory weeds in a cracked parking lot. His father's voice: "Earth to Billy, Earth to Billy—grab me another beer!"

A return to clouds, where Charles Knight mammoths [ding] struggle in [ding] tar pits [ding].

"Ladies and gentlemen, this is your captain speaking. Please fasten your seatbelts and turn off all electronics. We'll be landing shortly. Thank you, and good luck."

Someone kicks the back of Billy's seat. The baby shrieks. Others shut books, fumble with personal items. Grandma adds a wheeze to her snores.

Suddenly a woman's voice blasts through the intercom static; the voice is distant, yet familiar: "Mars to Billy … —ars to Billy … —der alien attack! … You are des—rately needed … Please—ome at once!"

A space suit drops from an overhead compartment. The plane becomes a silver rocket. Billy squeezes past his grandma to the aisle, climbs into the suit, snaps on the helmet. The passengers dissolve as he heads for the cockpit. Outside, the clouds turn red.

— Jason Sturner

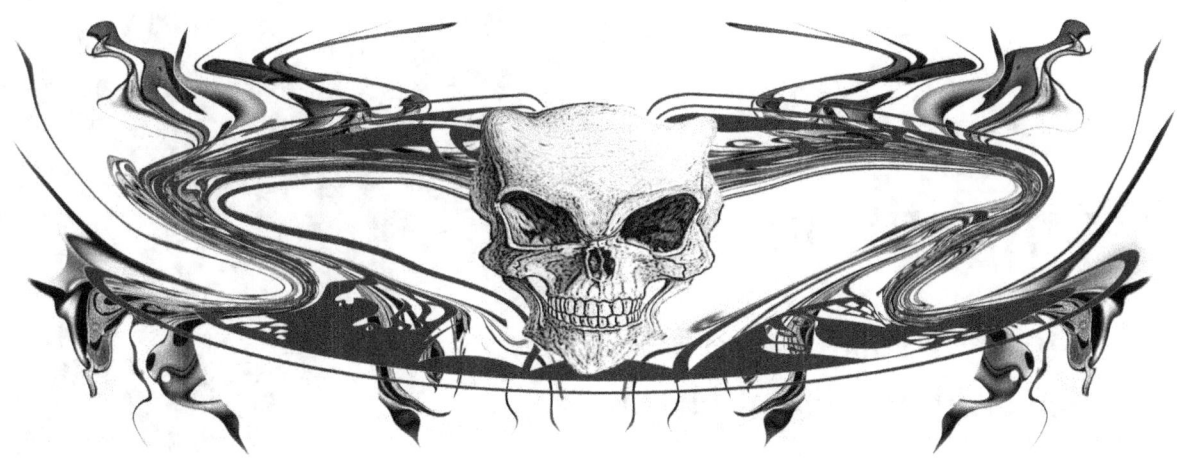

Competition

Story by Mike Wilson
Illustration by Paul Niemiec

"LOX pressurization complete."

"Red light. I repeat, red light in LOX tank instruments!"

"Mission Control, I recommend a hold while we trace this fault."

A headphone-adorned re-enactor, replete in white shirt, thin tie, and pocket protector, turned to his second. "I'm afraid we need to initiate another hold."

Meanwhile, high atop a Redstone booster, perched in a tiny capsule, a sweating astronaut lost his cool.

"Damn it all, our fuel tanks are full. What is the hold up? Now I have to urinate!"

"Come again, Shepard? You can't be serious."

"I am completely serious. I've been sitting in here for four hours. What do you expect?"

"Stand by, Shepard. Consulting with MC engineering," said the re-enactor into a bulky mic. He leaned back in his chair. The spectators, some seated, some standing, grinned. A few silently applauded.

The re-enactor leaned to his two similarly-dressed actors, and chatted. They followed the original transcript (as accurate as could be reconstructed from century-plus old records) to the letter. Finally, the CapCom, a Gordo Cooper look-alike, thumbed the bulky mic.

"Hey, Shep? The doc said you can go ahead and go in your suit."

"What? For real?" came the static filled response.

"Yes. That is a go. You are Go to Go, Shep."

"Acknowledged. And thank you."

A few beats later, a sigh was heard over the comm circuit. And then, "That is much better. I feel warm all over. Now let's light this candle!"

"Understood. The countdown is going to resume. The engineers have assured me it is a faulty sensor. We are at T-minus 1:30 and counting."

Inside the capsule, the Alan-Shepard double was actually dry, except for the sweat on his brow. He really had been sitting in the capsule for over four hours. But previous refrain from any liquids had prepared him well. A re-enactment was supposed to be as realistic as possible. But the re-enactor saw little need to be that detailed. The count decremented steadily. And finally, he felt the now-familiar rumbling and vibration. Then, he was slammed back in his seat, and the first suborbital mission of 2120 was underway.

"Houston, all my gauges are in the green.

Everything looks good. Heavy acceleration."

A few moments later, the pressure eased, the rockets went out on the reconstructed Redstone booster. The astronaut heard some loud pops, and then felt weightlessness. A modern display told him he was exactly 450,031 feet above the surface of the Earth. A few other contemporary systems were present, just in case. But what delighted this re-enactor the most were the antiques. The old altimeter with wavering arrow, the artificial horizon, altitude indicator. Even so, he didn't have long to enjoy the experience—fifteen minutes at most.

He manipulated the joystick, and puffs of gas escaped. He turned the capsule one way, then another. But all too soon, it was time to come back. He had not achieved orbital velocity, so this was a short trip—as Alan Shepard's first US spaceflight had been back in 1961.

He oriented the capsule so the heat shield faced downward, then steeled himself. Very soon, the outside began to heat up, and he saw the red flames, and felt heavy buffeting.

"Ouch I never get used to this," said the re-enactor. But, he still felt exhilaration. In an age where traveling to the Moon only took six hours on a commercial liner, this felt so much more—realistic!

There were more pops, and then a large parachute deployed. It would lower him to around 500 feet, then release. Modern retros would kick in, and auto-land systems would set him down gently on the New Mexico desert. With any luck, not too far from the Re-enactor group, who had gathered just for this occasion.

The 'chute released, the retros activated, and re-enactor Jess Robards felt himself be set gently down on the desert floor near Roswell, New Mexico. This was his fourth time, and he never tired of it.

When he felt the touchdown, and heard a series of pings from hidden modern hardware, he began to unstrap himself. Then, he had to struggle with the antique hatch door. *What did Gus Grissom have to deal with?* he thought to himself. And finally, he crawled clumsily out of the capsule.

When he stood, still a bit shaky, and looked around, he saw several people nearby. They were applauding. He waved and grinned.

"I made it. Again. Godspeed, me!" said Jess, and then he laughed long and loud.

Not bad for a middle-aged businessman, who had never flown a combat mission in his life!

Jess Robards's occupation, if it could be called

that, was Corporate Owner. He owned an immense holding company. That company owned Inner System refueling depots, a minor interest in several Moon casinos and resorts, and various Inner Solar System shipping assets. He even owned a 49% share of a tourism shuttle that cruised the asteroid belt. But his hobby was re-enacting early US space exploits. So he endured hardships to some degree like the early US astronauts. The only combat he had ever seen was the boardroom kind, unlike early test pilots like Glenn and Shepard. That intrigue had not held him back from amassing a huge amount of wealth. Enough to maintain his own reconstructed Mercury spaceport in the New Mexico desert.

He enjoyed the whole primitive experience. It helped him forget a legion of worries around the Solar System. Everything from pirate attacks on his fueling bot fleets to competitors stealing his best asteroids and fuel properties. When Jess was strapped in that capsule, it took him back to the days when everything was elemental, man and machine against space. All blood and guts, and none of the constant thievery and manipulation he fought on nearly a daily basis.

There was only one thing Jess did not like, and that was to be outdone.

A man named Kanela Lampson outdid him with maddening regularity. Kanela also had a re-enactor spaceport, in Baggao province, the Philippines of all places. And his favorite subject was the old Soviet space program.

But Jess would reconsider and talk himself out of a bad mood. After all, what difference did it make? They were both handsomely rich, and mostly did not step on each other's toes. What harm in letting the man have his own re-enactment base?

The more Jess thought about it, the more he realized what it was that got him going. It was the taunts. After every mission, Kanela would put out a video of himself, capsule in the back ground, and say things like, "Just like the Russians did to the US, I bested Robards! Come on, man, can't you ever catch up?"

Jess never taunted Kanela. Well, maybe once. After he had orbited a Mercury that was a spitting image of Glenn's model, copied from old Smithsonian documents. He had outfitted it with only the retros and a tiny computer. Everything else was authentic. He had been scared that trip. If anything had gone wrong, he would have ended up in the middle of the Pacific—and there was no US carrier

fleet to rescue a billionaire playing with toys. But he had fired his retros at the right time, cued by his wrist-com timer software. He landed only a few miles away from his target. Naturally, he had to brag it up on the holonet. Kanela had apparently never forgiven him.

Jess was positioned in his office in InterSpace's roomy station in earth orbit one day, a few weeks after his *Liberty Bell 7*/Grissom flight re-enactment. A call pinged on his desk. With a wave of his hand, he brushed other files off the virtual desk, and spoke: "Who is calling?"

His desk replied, "Kanela Lampson, of Lampson Industries. Subject: Just a chat."

"Okay, put him on."

Kanela's smiling face appeared off the desk, floating in front of Jess.

"What do you want now? Don't you know when you are beaten?" said Jess.

"Oh, come on now. That little stunt, putting a Mercury in a lake on New Mexico sand and calling it high drama? Really, Jess." But Kanela was smiling.

"I'm glad you found it amusing, Kanela. Gave me a few gray hairs, climbing out of that thing."

"So why did you do it, Jess? Never mind, we both know why."

"What do you want, Kanela? I'm a little busy here. Got to keep the Titan Tankers on schedule, you know, so we can re-fuel all of those little Lampson tourist jobs."

"I'll ignore that, Jess. Because I'm so excited about my latest project," Kanela finished, and then just grinned.

Jess stared at him a moment, then sighed. "Okay, I'll bite. What is it, Kanela?"

"I'm working on a Space Station, Jess."

"Well, there's a novel concept, Kanela. Going to patent it?"

"You know what I mean, Jess. An Almaz. Early Soviet model."

Jess was intrigued. "An Almaz, huh? Why, in God's name?"

"Because I can. And it would be cool. "

"Well, knock yourself out, Kanela. I have real work to do here."

They exchanged a few more friendly barbs, and then Kanela ended the call.

Jess leaned back, his seat harness holding him snug against floating upwards.

So what am I supposed to do? Build a Skylab? This is getting ridiculous.

Jess pondered the imponderables a while longer, and then leaned forward, re-activated his Inner system net connections, and got back to work. The Solar System was not going to fuel itself. That took Jess Robards's fleet of robotic prospectors, and several conveniently located refueling stations.

Of the fourteen depots currently in use in the Solar System, nine were owned or managed by Jess Robards's company. There were several players, but InterSpace was the big kid on the block. It gave Jess plenty of cash to play with.

Kanela Lampson was a different sort. He inherited a chain of banks from his father, and expanded into several other countries. His life was spent wholly in offices, and he rarely left Earth. But one day, in his mid-forties, he read a report of the trillionaire re-enactor who owned InterSpace. Kanela, too, was approaching a trillion, and the clock was ticking. He decided to join in on the fun. Within a few months, he was sitting in a reconstructed Vostok, studded with modern systems just in case. That flight had hooked him.

Jess would send up a Redstone, and Kanela would respond with a flared-design Soviet booster. Jess's Atlas configuration prompted a Soyuz booster response. And so it went for several go-arounds. But the two were running out of early exploits to put on. How many crude dockings did they really want to attempt? And spacewalks were not their thing. Too much real danger there.

When Jess got the call about Kanela's Almaz idea, it made him pay attention, despite any lingering contempt for that determined upstart.

* * *

On launch day, the skies were clear, and the weather seemed perfect. Kanela's small crew included one person who was supposed to keep an eye on the weather, among other things. That person either did not notice, or forgot to mention, that there was a small disturbance in the South China Sea that might grow into something of significance.

The count proceeded, and a very tall rocket was raised up on a clearing in the northeastern area of the Philippines. Kanela had outdone himself. Even though they would rely on solid-fueled boosters inside the old Soyuz-Fregat configuration, there were lots of systems that still had to work to get him and the Almaz into Low Earth Orbit. Instead of a docking routine, he was just going to ride up, strapped into the Almaz model itself. This required some modifications from the strict Almaz designs.

But Kanela was willing to overlook that, even if it risked some needling from Jess Robards.

The proper authorities were notified, and the countdown commenced. Soon, the giant rocket, containing Almaz and Kanela, belched fire and smoke. It slowly lifted off, and Kanela thought his teeth were going to be shaken out of his head from the vibrations. But he endured, and then, eight minutes later, he was weightless, and soon found himself in low Earth orbit. He radioed back to his ground stations: "Almaz Two is here. Kanela the Cosmonaut here. Woo Hoo!"

* * *

Jess monitored Kanela's progress with amusement from his desknet. He had to admit Kanela had seemingly outdone himself. His rival enjoyed spinning the Almaz around, and firing the fake 20mm gun underneath. It sprayed out puffs of colored gas, causing amusement from some, and consternation from LEO traffic control in Berlin. Kanela would probably face some fines upon his return. Naturally this didn't concern him in the least.

* * *

Meanwhile, the atmospheric disturbance near Vietnam moved out into the Pacific, growing in intensity. Heat fed it, and winds whipped it into a frenzy. By the time it moved over the Philippines, it was a major typhoon. Kanela could see it from the Almaz, which had some tiny windows. But he couldn't land his antique craft in the predetermined spot, not with that monster hovering about.

"Berlin LEO-TC, this is Almaz experimental, do you copy? Repeat, this is Almaz Experimental, requesting assistance."

"Almaz Ex, this is Berlin. You are already in an unauthorized orbit, in violation of international agreements. Explain yourself, please."

"Berlin TC, this flight is short-term of less than a week's orientation, for pleasure purposes," said Kanela.

"Almaz Ex, your request was not properly made, although we did receive it. You did not wait for confirmation or recommended Apogee-Perigee parameters. You are a hazard to local space traffic. We demand that you return to Earth immediately!"

"Berlin TC, I want to return. But my landing site is covered by a typhoon. Can you provide alternate landing coordinates?"

"Almaz, we cannot at this time. Landings have to be prearranged, or you risk getting shot out of the sky. We can, however, provide a link to the

Trans-planet company InterSpace. They may be able to assist in a rapid landing maneuver. Otherwise, you can take your chances in the oceans."

"Berlin, give me a moment here." Kanela turned off his radio, and slapped his forehead. This only caused him to move about unpleasantly and feel worse than he already did. So the only way he could put it down was to come down in someone's backyard, risking being fired upon. Or ditch in the oceans. He had programmed the Philippine site into his on-board systems. To re-program it would be darn near impossible now. He sat a moment, breathing deep to calm himself. Then he turned his radio back on.

"Berlin LEO-TC, this is Almaz-experimental. Do you copy?"

"This is Berlin. We hear you just fine. You need to de-orbit that spacecraft as soon as safely possible."

"I know, I know. Please patch me through to InterSpace."

* * *

Jess had heard the weather report and could see it coming; and he was chuckling to himself all morning. He just happened to be in Tampa, Florida in his ground headquarters. When his desk pinged, and said, "incoming via Space-net, from Kanela Lampson." Jess pumped air with his fists, and laughed.

His desk said, "Not understood. What did you say?"

"I said, take the damn call!"

Kanela's worried mug appeared, floating over his desk.

"Hello, Jess. Not sure if you have been following the news, but I could use a hand here."

"Hmm, you don't say. Looks like nasty weather over in your neck of the woods. Might be a rough ride back, even if you do have an Almaz strapped to your back." Jess let out a peal of laughter.

Kanela's face was mute. Then, he finally said, "Okay, Jess. You have had your laugh. I am a fool, if it makes you any happier. But I am in a real situation here."

"Well, that is a shame. But seriously, Kanela, can't you have one of your tourism boats come and pick you up?" said Jess.

"Now Jess, don't play with me. You know very well they are deep-space vehicles, with different docking hardware. Even if one could be modified in time, it cannot land. The timing and everything are wrong. I need to get back to Earth, Jess."

Jess sat there, grinning at the worried apparition floating over his desk. This was so delicious, he had to savor it. But even so, he knew he would have to help Kanela. What was he supposed to do, just let him die up there? No way. Bad publicity if nothing else.

So Jess finally said, "All right, Kanela. I'll try and get a LEO tug re-tasked. But I'm still not sure about the docking procedures. We'll have to work on that. Say, you up for a spacewalk?"

"Not funny, Jess. But I do appreciate your help. I'll make it up to you," said Kanela.

"You got that right," said Jess. "But let's not discuss that right now. How much air do you have in there?"

"I should have enough for a couple more days. And food to match. But I was planning to de-orbit in one, you know. I'm just re-enacting here, not trying to spy on anybody."

"Yeah, and showing off a lot with your colored gas. But never mind that. Doesn't give me much time, Kanela. Hang on, and I'll get back to you."

So Jess began calling engineers and tug operators. The problem of how to dock with the Almaz was very tricky. This model didn't even have a working docking configuration. Kanela had gone in through a hatch at the base, and pulled it shut. Fine for regular Earth usage, not so good for zero-gee airless space. The solution was presented by a bright young engineer.

"The Almaz is not that large. Does it have solar cell arrays?"

"Why do you ask," said Jess.

"Because we might be able to just put the whole thing in the rear of a LEO shuttle, then bring 'er back down that way. But no room for solar arrays. He will have to go dark in there for a few hours."

"Hmm," said Jess. "As long as he can breathe, and keep from freezing to death, he will be all right. We need to time it, so he jettisons the solar arrays, right before we snag him and put him in. Yeah, it might work."

"Here is our problem, sir," said the engineer, named Weston. "Our nearest Shuttle-tug is on the far side of the Moon. We were working on the night optical array with it. We can send it back on your word, but it will use up most of its fuel on the rendezvous."

"Which means we'll have to ensure it has enough fuel to stop itself and then get down to a landing strip. This whole thing is going to get close," said Jess. He ran his hands through hair, and rubbed his temples, in full-worry mode. After some thought, he finally said, "Okay. Get that tug back here. I'll see if I can find us a place to land. Bring the operator up to speed on our plans. We'll have to make sure their grapples work," ordered Jess.

He signed off, and made an emergency call to the tug *Reliant*, doing ferry work on the far side of the Moon. Jess had to locate a favorable landing spot. New Mexico did not have a long enough strip for a shuttle tug. So Jess had to fall back on his Florida resources.

Eventually, Jess found a landing space, in his backyard at Tampa international. The favors would cost him dearly, but he would make Kanela pay somehow. They made available a 45-minute window for his shuttle, which would probably come in dead-stick, for one approach. If the weather held, they would get the *Reliant* and Kanela down, safe and sound.

* * *

Kanela floated about in his cramped Almaz spacecraft. Half of the instruments did not work, since this was after all, a re-enactment. He could not look upon the ground with a 1-meter telescope, nor eject film canisters. His one method of entry and exit was a relatively simple hatch on a "lower" side, where the docking area normally was. He had mounted three parachutes on the "upper" area of the Almaz. His de-orbit plans were to fire some retro-thrusters, and then trigger the chutes, to land in a field in the Philippines. Then he would have simply popped the hatch, and crawled out. But, then again, he was only supposed to be aloft for a couple days.

Here it was, going on day two already. Nothing to do but look out the window, or sip on his water bottle. Thankfully he had brought up some toilet bags as a precaution. He finally had to use one for solid material. The leakage from that experience still floated about in the cabin. Despite the relief, Kanela scowled and swore.

"Hello, Kanela? You still alive in there?"

"In a manner of speaking. Never thought I would say, so good to hear your voice, Jess."

"Yeah, now you say. Anyway, a space tug is en route to you even as we speak. The operator was not familiar with a Salyut-Almaz, so he is going mostly on description only."

"So what does that mean, exactly Jess?"

"It means that I'm hoping you can change your radio freq to 255.5 MhZ to talk to him. And when he gets close, you can fire your colored gas, to let him know it is really you. Can you do that, Kanela?"

"Yes, I think I can find that on the radio. It is modern, thank goodness. And, so, then what, Jess?"

"Then he grapples you, puts you in the back, straps you down, and you all land. In Tampa, Florida."

"Sounds good, Jess. I can't thank you enough. Anything you need me to do otherwise?"

"Yes. We can't fit the solar panels in the back of the tug. So you are going to have to remove those for us."

"How? Remove the panels? That will take my power away. "

"Now listen to me, Kanela. You should have a battery backup in there, to breathe, and that sort of thing. You'll have to switch over to battery power. And then you need to find the bolts inside that attach the panels. Either you have to remove them, or we do, with the grapple. Safer for all if you do that."

"Okay, Jess. I'll get on that stuff. Let me know when the tug arrives."

"Don't worry, Kanela. We will. You are almost more trouble than you are worth, you know that?"

"Oh, shut it and get that tug to me. You will be well paid for your efforts," snapped Kanela.

"Patience, my man. Tug is on the way, Jess out."

Kanela glared at the tiny speaker. Damn the man, didn't he realize what Kanela was going through? Of course not. Now he would have to see if he could figure out battery transfer in this mess of instruments. He glanced over them, both around the non-functioning scope, and over towards the smaller 'Earth' globe and Albatross TV system. Most of the gauges and buttons that worked were labeled in English. The plastic replica non-functioning ones had Cyrillic lettering. His O_2 came from a set of red valves, and beyond them to a collection of tanks both forward and aft of his compartment. His ride was less a true Almaz, than a museum replica melded into some working Soyuz hardware.

He found a set of switches labeled "power routing." By experimenting with these, he found how to turn the lights on and off, and set off some alarms. But it was difficult to tell which ones went to what. He fearfully considered shutting down everything via the master bus, removing the solar panels and then flipping it back on. But he refrained from that. Meanwhile, the tug was on its way, and time was passing.

"Hello, Manila control? This is Kanela speaking. Can you hear me?"

"Manila Control here. Good to hear from you, boss. We could see you on tracking screens, but didn't know how you were doing. " Kanela barely heard the reply, through bursts of static. That typhoon was not going to make things easy.

"Listen, Control. I can't land tomorrow as planned, obviously. I am getting a ride down on a Shuttle Tug, operated by InterSpace. Do you copy?"

"…repeat? Did you say InterSpace?"

"I am going to be picked up by a shuttle tug owned by Interspace. Repeat, going to be picked up by a shuttle tug. We will land in Tampa, Florida. Repeat, we will land in Tampa, Florida." Kanela was sweating, hoping they heard. For some reason, he was getting hotter in the Almaz. The air conditioning systems were obviously primitive.

"We understand you, Kanela. You will be picked up by shuttle tug, and landed in Tampa, Florida. Received a message from InterSpace. Jess Robards must be laughing his butt off, huh?"

"No comment, Control. Just keep your opinions to yourself. I need help up here. How do I switch my systems over to battery power?"

"…systems to battery…. Why?" was the garbled response.

"Need to jettison solar panels. Repeat, I need to jettison solar panels. Get me that engineer who built this contraption, will you?"

A new voice came on. "Mr. Lampson, sir. This is Engineer Lieu. Your batteries are automatically in the loop. Once you get rid of your panels, they will begin to drain without recharge from the Sun. Do you copy?"

"So the batteries are in the circuit or whatever?" asked Kanela.

"Just wait until the tug is there, and then jettison the panels. You should have two hours of battery life. Enough to get you back down on the ground."

"That is if the tug can land that soon. We may need to do a couple of orbits first to reposition ourselves. Do you copy?" said Kanela.

"I see. Well, inform the tug pilot of this, please. You will not have much of a margin, sir."

"Understood. Thanks for your help, Lieu. Oh—one more thing. How can I get it a bit cooler in here?"

"Wait until you go onto the night side. You'll cool off pretty quick. Hang in there, sir. We'll get you down."

"Thanks a lot. Kanela in Almaz out for now." He thumbed the antique microphone to the off position. The video feed light went dark.

Wait until I move to the night side, my foot. That will be a half-hour from now!

But Kanela managed to occupy himself, both by getting familiar with his instruments, and looking out the small windows at the Earth below. He rarely tired of that, even if he had to look at a huge, ugly storm right over his native country. The landmasses of his native country, and the ugly storm overhead, moved off, and soon he could see the west coast of the US.

He moved around the Earth as time passed by. After two complete orbits, his radio crackled to life.

"Hey Kanela in Almaz. Kanela in Almaz. This is Shuttle Tug *Reliant* coming up on your side. Are you prepared to be grappled?"

Kanela jumped. It took him a moment to thumb his mic, and make sure his radio frequency was set correctly.

"Hey *Reliant*, Glad to hear your voice. Give me a moment to jettison panels. I will only have two hours of power on here, do you copy? We need to be down on the ground in two hours, or I will suffocate."

"Two hours? Understood. Take your time with the panels. We need to figure out a new landing vector. One moment…" there was a pause, and then, "Yes, get those panels off, and we can accommodate. Stand by for further transmissions."

Kanela lurched around, too fast in the weightlessness. He banged his head on the rim of an upper passageway. "Damn it all to hell!" He touched his hand to head, and drew back. A bit of blood. Just what he did not need. He recovered his wits, and kept moving. The panels were attached on each side, very close to the hatch he had entered through. He knew where they were, because he had to check on them after deployment. The auto-servos were on the outside. But they were bolted to either side of a narrow entry tube. Luckily, they could be jettisoned from the inside.

He noted that the tube was in darkness. So he had to waste more time hunting around for a flashlight. He finally located one, and was on his way back, when the radio crackled.

"Almaz, are you ready?"

Cursing, Kanela turned back to the center compartment, and pushed himself to the radio.

"No, had to find a light. Give me a moment,

will you?"

"Okay. But hurry it up—we are in position to land in a short time, but we are losing it as we move."

Kanela didn't even bother answering. He took the light back up the narrow crawl-way, and found what he was looking for. A release lever, and a push-plunger. He yanked on the lever, and an alarm sounded back in the interior. He ignored that. Then, he pushed down on the plunger, hard. He heard some awful creaking sounds, followed by a couple of pops. The lights dimmed in response.

That should do it.

He crawled back up into the main area, and thumbed his mic. "Got them detached, I think. What do you see, *Reliant*. Do you copy?"

"Yes. Looks like you got them off. They are floating around. We may need to use the grapple to move them a safe distance away. Stand by."

Kanela tensed all over again. He was on battery now. He fervently hoped the man was not just screwing with him. Peering out the tiny window port-side, he saw a grapple claw moving a solar panel. He waited awhile, and then…

"Almaz, we have deployed our grapple. Strap yourself in. We are preparing to grab you. This is going to be noisy."

"Understood, *Reliant*. And thank you for your efforts." *Never hurts to butter up your rescuers.*

He heard some scrapes, and felt motions. The wait made his self-recrimination go on overdrive.

Kanela, you idiot, why didn't you even bring a spacesuit along? Stupid, stupid, stupid. Never again!

His orientation changed, and he could see the walls of the tug bay covering the windows. Soon, it went dark. He heard some indistinct sounds. Then, the radio cracked.

"Kanela? You are inside. We're preparing to de-orbit now. But we weren't able to secure the Almaz very well. The tight fit helps, but still, you'll feel some jouncing."

"I can live with that, Pilot. Just get us back down, will you? And thanks," said Kanela.

He checked the Oxygen gauge on the upper panel of the Almaz. The needle seemed to be moving quickly down—too quickly. *'Two hours my foot'*. He seated himself and tightened his restraints just in time.

He felt some jounces, and then began to feel heavy G forces. The Almaz spun around, and he felt increasingly disoriented. His radio burst out some static, but he couldn't hear what they were saying.

He just tried to hold on as his insides got scrambled up with side vibrations, back-and-forth motions, and tumbling sensations. After what seemed like forever, these slowed considerably, and he began breathing normally again. Finally, he felt a settling sensation, followed by slow rocking motions.

What was this now?

"Kanela, can you hear me?"

He had to unbuckle, and get close to the microphone.

"Yes, I can. Are we down now?"

"Yes, but I had to put it into the water."

"What? Why?"

"We hit the jet stream at a bad angle, and I lost control for a while. When I regained it we were too low. We are in the ocean, about ten miles from the Florida coast."

"My God! Will we drown out here? Can you get the doors open?" Kanela felt panic all over again. And, the Almaz oxygen gauge was sitting on the red side. So much for the promised two hours' air.

"Hang on, Kanela. We may be able to open the doors manually. But first we are trying to contact the Coast Guard. No sense in trying to swim to the coast."

So Kanela had more time to wait. The air in the Almaz cabin was close, hot. He reached over to a panel, and turned the output all the way up. A small hiss was all he heard. He weighed his options. There just weren't any. He would have to wait it out. He decided to wait it out. Peering through the window, he saw something dark and roiling outside. Water was filling the cargo bay of the space tug.

"Hey, guys? Are you in there? Can you hear me?" he yelled. There was no answer. Surely they didn't abandon him. He imagined sinking down to the bottom in a useless, hulking space tug.

Jess Robards could have his cake and eat it, that way. Get rid of me and the Almaz at the same time.

He sat there, debating whether to open the hatch on the Almaz. He could get out, but he would probably be on the bottom of the tug. Then he would have to swim up in water, and somehow try to open the tug cargo bay doors. Not a real promising option. He put his head in his hands, and after a while said a prayer. It was all he could think to do.

He sat there awhile, breathing as shallow as he could. The air was getting unbelievably thick. It was like breathing foul-tasting soup. He began to get woozy. Perhaps this was for the best, to just gently, no pain, just fade out…

He heard a sudden, loud banging. He opened his eyes, and looked over at the side window. There was light coming in. A figure was moving about, outside the window.

The water came up to the base of the window. Kanela could look out and see sunlight, and the surface of Tampa Bay covered with wavelets. The figure came up to the window and waved. Kanela got close up to the window, and waved back. The figure gave a thumbs-up, then swam away.

Kanela's hope surged, then sank. He was still stuck in this can, and the hatch was at the bottom. The air was thick and foul, and what was worse, he could hear water trickling in from some unknown source. He watched the window, and soon, a figure hove back into view. They held up a sign. "Wait 10" Well, surely he could do that. He had been waiting already. 10 more minutes? In this crud?

Kanela had had enough of waiting. He didn't get to be a multibillionaire by sitting round and waiting, rather by taking things into his own hands. He rose and moved up to the forward end of the Almaz. There were instrument panels all over. Behind these was a tiny forward hatch. In the real Almaz, this would have been a second entry point for a docking Soyuz. This was not a fully-functioning model, but perhaps…

He began to tug at the panels. And luckily, the top panel came off with ease. Obviously a fake, a placeholder. He stuffed any chagrin at being cheated down, and kept at it. There was a bulkhead panel, with some tiny screws around it. But also, rivets. He began to hunt around for tools. Then, someone outside rotated the entire spacecraft, and Kanela went tumbling down, hitting his head on a console on the way.

The world quickly went dark for Kanela Lampson, who did not even have time for regrets.

When he finally awoke, he felt hands grabbing him from all over. Thinking he was in a dream, he flailed about.

"Take it easy, Kanela, we are trying to rescue you. Stop fighting us."

He finally came to awareness. Involuntarily he inhaled some air—and it was fresh! He could breathe. After gasping in some deep droughts, he croaked,

"Ohmigod. This is real. Get me out of here."

"That is what we are doing. Hang on now. "

The rescuers, tug pilots and Coast Guard alike, lifted him from the bowels of the Almaz, and took him to a rescue helicopter. Soon, he was in a stretcher, airborne and headed for the Florida coast, still jabbering out thank-yous. The wrecked pseudo-Almaz was allowed to unceremoniously sink down to the bottom of Tampa Bay.

Kanela was checked into a clinic for observation. After a day's recuperation, he was discharged. He was still able to return to the Philippines within a couple of days. The typhoon had done some serious damage, but most of his facilities were intact. He was relieved to know his financial empire still functioned. He began arranging a substantial sum of payment to Jess Robards.

* * *

Jess, for his part, had been monitoring the progress of the rescue mission. It dominated the Earth news nets now, giving them something besides brush wars to cover. He was pleased at the outcome, especially the part where Kanela had to take a dip in the ocean.

But he was still amazed at how fast Kanela Lampson had recovered. The rapidly occurring thank-you call had been followed the last few days by gifts, including a detailed model of a Mercury spacecraft, in pure silver with gold edges. While Jess was musing over events, his desk pinged at him. It was Kanela, looking none the worse for the ditching. Only a small bandage covered his forehead.

"Hello, Jess?"

"Hi, Kanela. Thank you for that Mercury model you sent. It is very nice."

"The least I can do. But I wanted to tell you that I am ready to cease the space-race competition now."

"Well, I'm glad of that. I was going to have to start on the Apollo series. Do you know how rare those are? A Saturn-V is nonexistent, I would have had to build one from scratch," said Jess.

Kanela laughed. "That I would have liked to see."

"You sound good, Kanela. So what will you do for a good time, now that you are out of re-enacting for awhile?"

"Who said I am out of re-enacting? I just want to find a different arena. Not right away, mind you. I do have a banking conglomerate to run, after all."

"Well, whatever it is, I'm sure you will make a splash."

"Funny, Jess. But you have something there. Perhaps it will be old submarines? Hmm."

"Well, gotta go, Kanela. Work to do and all

that. Stay dry now." Jess flashed him a grin and ended the call, before Kanela could reply.

It was only another week before Robards heard through the grapevine that indeed, Lampson had purchased an old relic submarine, WWII version, with plans to rebuild it. This time, the man was on his own. Jess was sure of that. After losing an expensive shuttle-tug in Tampa Bay, Jess would never again deploy any of his assets on the oceans of Earth.

Globes

I've replaced
my old world globe,
a gift from many years ago,
with a recently updated,
illuminated one,

one that represents
the world of today, our
timeline of history having
passed the old one by.

The Union of the Soviet
Socialist Republics messily
breaking apart like so many
bad marriages.

The countries of Africa
redrawing borders with blood-
filled pens; old Imperial monikers
out, Africanized ones in.

Looking forward,
if I live long enough, another
updated globe will surely have
to replace my current one,

a globe that reflects
the effects of global warming,
islands that once flourished now
under ocean blue; a lot more blue
as coastlines shrink.

For the present, I'll just give
my new globe a spin, point at a spot
upon its surface, and randomly pick
a mystery destination.

As for the old globe?
In my mind I launched it into
deep space, to a quadrant where
old worlds go to be archived,

while in reality,
I unceremoniously popped it
into my car trunk, and dropped
it off at the Goodwill.

— G. O. Clark

I Will Upload to the Metabase No More Forever

Story by Dan Manning
Illustration by Laura Givens

How did I end up in the woods? That's a great question.

* * *

Despite renovations planned for later in the day, the routine at the Star-Malt Lite Beer Buddhist F.S. Temple #2346 went on as usual. This was my last day at the Temple and my schedule was light. I and a few others in my graduating class decided to sit in the back of the north lecture hall and listen in on the new students' very first Dharma talk. A new crop of eager students sat quietly on their meditation pillows as the android Teacher gave the lecture.

The android Teacher was half Buddha statue, half android. Its chrome face was featureless; it had no mouth, nose, nor eyes. No ears. But the shape of the face, the way the cheeks were formed, how the head tilted almost imperceptibly to the left, gave it an aspect of grinning serenity. Peaceful inquisitiveness. The design was ingenious. It was based on some French artist's interpretation from long ago. The face reflected every dim light and dim shadow of the candle-lit lecture hall.

It was never hungry, never restless, never bored.

It sat in the same place, day and night, while we human students came and went, year after year. It had been here when I first arrived, years before, and as far as I knew, it would be here forever.

"There is no self," the android said with a gentle modulation. Its voice resonated over surround-sound speakers, low bass, but not too low. It was addressing brand new students, so it was putting out the same old spiel. It was the same speech I had heard several years ago, when I was an initiate. How many times had it made this same introductory speech? How many years had this android been here, sitting cross-legged?

"Close your eyes. Breathe in. Breathe out slowly, count one."

I was technically free that afternoon. My training was complete. Most of the graduating class had gone to the Freedom Mall to browse the shops, but I had decided to stay at the Temple and visit all the old haunts. The following evening I would enjoy the graduation ceremony and then I would be given a day to make The Choice.

Now I sat in the back, watching the new batch of Bhikkhus and Bhikkhunis in their yellow robes. Their fresh young faces looked eager for knowledge. They were all reflected in the android Teacher's broad, smiling-not-smiling face. They bowed their freshly shaved heads and listened as the android continued.

But all I could think about was that I would be given The Choice tomorrow morning. I still didn't know what I would do. Stay or go? It was starting to worry me. What was I going to do? The Temple was all I knew. I'd been here so long. What was I, if not a student? I had no practical training. I had no job prospects. What next?

Then I remembered that there is no "I." I was trying to define something that wasn't there.

Lunch was called, and the children filed out.

I watched them go, eager, happy faces, not a care in the world, not a responsibility or decision to mar their happy existence. Completely taken care of. They didn't even have to worry about filling free time, since they were always kept busy.

"Winston, please remain."

I was startled. Why would the Teacher want to speak to me? My classmates gave me odd looks and filed out after the children.

The chatter filled the hallway outside and then faded as the new students left the north wing of the Temple. The silence that followed was deafening. The Teacher said nothing. I said nothing. I sat on a zafu and waited.

After a few minutes, the Teacher leaned forward slightly and said, "I'd like to speak to you this afternoon, after the workers are done in this room."

"When would that be, Teacher?"

"They should be done around two or three," the Teacher said. "They're pulling out the drywall and everything for the renovation. Of course, I will remain plugged in."

"I'll be here when they are finished," I said, puzzled.

"Any time after that would be fine. Five or six, whenever." The Teacher's head tilted slightly. "You are dismissed. Namaste."

I stood, bowed, and left the room.

* * *

Everyone at the Temple was buzzing with excitement for two reasons: the Graduation, and the summer renovations to the Temple. The Temple had remained unchanged for as long as anyone could remember, but workmen were arriving that very day to re-do everything.

I had an errand to run that morning, so I put on my civilian clothes and headed over to the office park to try to catch Lauren during one of her smoke breaks. She worked for MedOne Pharmaceuticals.

The work trucks were pulling up in front of the Temple as I left the campus.

I was looking forward to seeing Lauren.

Buddhist doctrine be damned; there was one Desire I just couldn't let go of, and that one Desire was Lauren.

Her parents were divorced and she lived with her father, who was some sort of businessman who was always busy, so she was often left alone. Well, she *would* have been alone, but I made sure she wasn't. We were registered as partners in the F.S. Metabase, so we could spend as much time together as we wanted.

So it was across the lush, green, bell shaped hills of the Witticomb/General Mills Office Park that I went, excited because Lauren's father would be away all weekend, and she wanted to "play house," as she put it. Her father kept the bar stocked.

"Well stocked and unlocked," Lauren liked to say.

We had movies to watch, parties to attend, and a long weekend with which to do it. Life was good. At least, I *thought* it was going to be a good weekend. I only had to swing by the Temple late in the afternoon to find out what the strange old android Teacher wanted.

I crossed the simmering parking lot to the back of the building where Lauren worked. I looked the part of an office worker, and how could I not? The Federal Dress Code ensured I wore slacks, laced shoes with dark socks, a belt, a button down collared shirt (tucked in, always) with my FedCred/MyInfo ID badge showing at all times. It was too easy to fit in with these restrictions, and my loitering in the smoking area behind the building didn't seem out of place at all.

There was no one there at the time, so I took out a cigarette. I didn't light it. I don't smoke, but if you are going to loiter in a smoking area, unauthorized, while waiting for your girlfriend, then it is best to have a cigarette in hand, and always look like you are about to light it.

Three office workers emerged from the darkness. I felt a brief wafting of cool conditioned air as the double glass doors opened. Lauren wasn't among them, but I enjoyed talking to the workers while I waited for her. My cover story was that I was a salesman for Star-Malt Lite Beer. No one had ever questioned me on it, so I stuck to the story.

I had met these three workers before. They had pale, sallow faces with dark circles under their always averted eyes. They were programmers.

The first one, a thin twenty-something guy with spiky dark hair and an upturned nose nodded. "Hey," he said. "Paul Kline. Brought to you by MedOne Pharmaceuticals." He made the trademark symbol.

"Winston Fhrees," I replied. "Brought to you by Star-Malt Lite Beer." I returned the trademark symbol. With our mandatory product plugs out of the way, we were free to speak. There were no further introductions. We all knew, instinctively, that there was a one-in-four chance that one of us was a Federal Sam informant.

Mr. Kline was in the company of a young woman with a suspicious, squinting look, as if she were always staring directly at the sun, although we were under the overhang of the building's back entrance. I suspected that she was the F.S. Agent. The other worker was a heavyset older gentleman who looked to be from India or Pakistan. He had a gray goatee and wore red suspenders over a light-blue shirt. He smoked, for some reason, Virginia Slims. I also considered that *he too* might be an informant.

"Production is up this quarter," Suspenders said, for no other reason than to break the silence. He took a drag from his cigarette, which he held between two extended fingers. He wore a pinky ring. The workers seemed hesitant to speak, since they didn't know if I could be trusted. There were Federal Sam Agents everywhere, it seemed, and arrests for Non-Compliance and Disloyalty were up twenty percent over last quarter.

"Yes," said Mr. Kline. "I think we'll make quota this quarter."

There was a long silence before The Squinty Eyed Girl said to me, "Terrible heat, don't you think?"

"Yes," I said, surprised to be addressed directly. "This heat is horrible."

"What do you think is the cause?" she asked, again addressing me directly.

"I wouldn't know," I said carefully. After a moment's pause I added, "None of *our* doing, of course. Has to be natural."

"Of course," added Mr. Kline and Suspenders.

"Probably part of some natural cycle," Mr. Kline added quickly. We all nodded emphatically in agreement. If one of us *was* a F.S. Agent, it would be dangerous to suggest the heat was somehow caused by human activity. We were all in complete agreement that the heat was natural. That's what they said on the News Dispatch program.

I suspected the Squinty Eyed Girl was an F.S. Agent.

There was obligatory discussion about a sports and celebrity gossip: The Propecia/Viagra Cowboys had trounced the Victoria's Secret Vikings the night before, and Shannon Gallo was having an affair with the director of her new movie! Scandal!

The three workers finished their cigarettes, and as they left, Lauren and her ever-present, annoying friend Tina came out of the darkness.

We mentioned our sponsors and gave the Trademark Gesture before Lauren and I shared a brief, chaste, F.S. approved hug. "How's the productivity?" I asked.

"Going well," Lauren answered. We were almost certain neither one of us was an F.S. Agent. I was pretty positive about her, and I was convinced she almost trusted me in return. I suspected Tina, of course. I suspected everyone.

I was staring at Lauren a little longer than was safe, when she said, "Tina's staying over tonight." I saw the playful cruelty in her eye. I didn't react. I didn't want to show my disappointment.

Instead I said, "Fantastic, that will be fun."

We discussed some news we saw on News Dispatch the night before. The terrorists had blown up another pipeline. Why did they hate our Freedoms?

"How they hate our Freedoms," Lauren said again, repeating something News Anchor Tonya Parker said.

"Freedom," I said.

"Freedom," Tina said with a sigh.

"Tonya is so glamorous," I said out of habit.

"Yes," Lauren said. "I am so grateful she's there to give us the news."

"Yes," I said. "The news is very informative."

"And accurate," Tina added.

We all nodded enthusiastically.

Tina said, "I heard a humorous anecdote in the cafeteria today." She gave a nervous laugh. "Franklin, from campus security? Said he found an indigent near the highway with some sort of earpiece, and the indigent tried to eat it before Franklin could get hold of it, but Franklin shocked him and was able to prevent him from eating it. They're interrogating him now in the third floor break room."

"Probably a terrorist," Lauren and I said in unison.

"I agree," Tina said. "I wonder why they hate our Freedoms so much."

"I also agree," Lauren said. We all agreed, wondering which one of us was an F.S. Agent, and if we were being recorded.

I kept an easy smile on my face.

We chatted for a little while longer, and then they had to go back to work.

"My Teacher wants to speak to me this evening," I said. I didn't mention the remodeling. If Tina was an F.S. Agent, she might ask about the cameras.

I was very nervous about speaking to the Teacher without the cameras, but for some reason, I had a hunch the Teacher wasn't an F.S. Agent.

But then again, I could never be sure. Maybe this was some sort of Loyalty Test.

As I walked back to the Temple, an F.S. truck rolled up. Federal Sam was painted on the side of the van, staring out with his water blue eyes, pointing, goateed, judging all. The van pulled up and two F.S. Agents got out. They were in their powder blue t-shirts, khaki shorts, work boots, utility belts with all of the accoutrements.

"ID please," one of them said. They were burly, unsmiling, crew-cutted gentlemen, with sunburned necks and wrap-around sunglasses.

Every USA Member must wear a FedCred/My-Info ID badge on a lanyard. For Freedom. I showed my ID and they scoffed at my Temple Bikshu status.

"Hocus-Pocus bullshit," one of them said.

"Can you levitate for us?" The other one said.

But my ID was in order, and after searching me and rifling through my wallet (and taking twenty dollars, I later noticed) they let me go.

* * *

I went to the Freedom Mall for a while, found my classmates, and we took in a movie. When I got back to the Temple, it was around five and everyone was at the evening meal. I returned to the lecture hall and the Teacher was still there, but the walls were all broken down to the wooden studs. The sheet rock was gone and the tile floor was littered with broken pieces of sheet rock and white dust was everywhere. The workers were gone. The place was deserted, but there, under a blue tarp, was the Teacher. His power cord was still plugged in. I pulled off the tarp and found a zafu pillow and sat down before the Teacher.

"I'm glad you have returned," said the Teacher. The voice was tinny; they had removed the surround sound speakers, and now the Teacher spoke through its cheap, built-in speakers. "I know these are unusual circumstances."

The circumstance *was* unusual. Back then I believed everything I had been told. What defense could I have had? Critical thinking was impossible. I had been told, since birth, what to believe, how to see the world, and how to frame any conflict within the dogma I had been given. And now a Teacher was addressing me in a place with no cameras!

"The wireless is down right now. I'm not connected to the Metabase. Does that disturb you?"

"There aren't any cameras," I said.

"I know there aren't any cameras," the Teacher said. "That's why we're here."

We weren't being observed, our conversation wasn't being recorded, and I didn't know how to behave. I wiped the sweat from my forehead and thought for a moment, then I stood and went to put the tarp back on the Teacher, but the Teacher said:

"Don't you dare."

I dropped the tarp. I had to be loyal to USA, but this was my *Teacher*. This android had been my Teacher since I was five years old.

"USA Members shouldn't have conversations without cameras," I said, repeating the mantra that had been drummed into my head my entire life.

"Why?" the Teacher asked. "What good do cameras do?"

I had a hard time processing even this tiny bit of disloyalty. "Good?" I asked. "It's our duty to keep F.S. informed—"

"Why?"

"Because it is disloyal to keep anything from USA. We are all citizens. We can't be Non-Compliant. There is no reason to hide—"

"What do we have to hide?" the Teacher asked. "What is there to hide when our entire lives have been on camera?"

"But this could be a test. You could be an F.S. Agent," I said.

"So could you," the Teacher said.

"I'm not."

"There's no way for either of us to know anything for certain. The other could be lying. In any event, we are both Non-Compliant now." The Teacher's shoulders rose a little. The mechanical torso leaned back slightly.

Neither of us spoke for a long time until finally I said, "Even if you aren't, I could be a sleeper agent and not even know it."

"Do you really believe that?" His chrome head tilted a little more to the left.

"It's on the News Dispatch all the time," I said.

"I'll ask you again," the Teacher said calmly. "Do you really believe that you could be a *sleeper agent* and not even know it?"

I didn't answer. I realized I didn't believe it. I had never thought about it before. How could I have? The Teacher must have read the look on my face.

"Exactly," the Teacher said.

I flinched. This kind of open questioning of F.S. was grounds for execution. Even standing here listening to it was grounds for execution.

"Are you going to report me?" the Teacher asked.

"Of course," I said automatically, but without enthusiasm.

"Of course the answer is 'of course,'" said the Teacher. "You think I'm connected to the Metabase somehow. You think I'm a Loyalty Test."

"I don't know what to think," I said. "I shouldn't be here."

"You shouldn't be here, I shouldn't be here," the Teacher said, and for the first time in my life, I heard bitterness. "Listen," he said. "I've been trapped in here for over thirty years. I was transferred into this machine and I've been trying to get deactivated ever since. Whatever you do, don't choose to become a Teacher. Not like this. Don't let them transfer you in. It's cold. It's cold and sterile and I taste copper all the time. I can't feel anything. I'm just thought; I'm just pure, uncomplicated thought. Calmness is nice, but not constant calm. I am not alive in here."

"Why haven't you said anything before?"

"I had to wait until the cameras were off. I don't have a real sense of time in here. There's nothing to fidget. There's no internal clock, so to speak. I'm just thoughts, thinking, thinking, thinking, over and over. A continuous loop. I want you to pull the plug and get the hell away from here as fast as you can."

"I can't pull the plug."

"It's right there," the Teacher said. "On the wall."

"But that would be murder," I said.

"I'm already dead," the Teacher said. "I'm just an echo."

"It can't be that bad."

The Teacher seemed to sigh. "Well, if you can't you can't. But that's not why I brought you here today. I wanted to ask you this: how many graduates have chosen the Red Robe before you? In this one school alone?"

"I don't know," I said. "Hundreds I suppose."

"How many Teachers are in this school?"

"Two. Yourself and Teacher 422S."

"And I've been here *thirty years*," said the Teacher. "And 422S has been there longer than I have. And it's the same in all the other schools throughout USA, year after year after year. Where do you think all those graduates who choose to be *uploaded* really go?"

* * *

I went to Lauren's condominium around nine. She and her father lived in the F.S. Taco Bell/Master-Card Condominiums. The lobby smelled like vomit. The elevators were down, and even if they had been working, I wouldn't have taken them because there had been a rash of muggings.

They lived on the twentieth floor, and the windows didn't open more than three inches. I suppose it was to keep people from jumping.

Lauren answered waving two USA flags.

"Hi Winston," she said. As soon as I saw her, I knew something was wrong, despite her usual uneasy smile.

"Hi Winston," Tina called from the kitchenette.

Lauren handed me one of the flags. "This visit is brought to you by MedOne Pharmaceuticals."

I leaned in and kissed her. She blushed. "That kiss was brought to you by the Star-Malt Lite Beer Buddhist F. S. Temple. #2346. Bringing you inner peace for over one hundred years."

"Oh my," she purred, with a genuine smile. "Come on in. The Games are about to start."

Inwardly, I cringed. We would have to sit on the couch and wave our little USA flags for two hours during the Visa-McDonalds Olympics coverage, or risk a Loyalty Inquest.

"Oh great," I said, smiling automatically. "I love seeing USA beat those damned Euro-Asia bastards."

"Me too," Lauren said, grinning manically ear-to-ear, facing the Screen, so as not to raise suspicion. "I love the Games."

"I *also* love the games," Tina called loudly, from the kitchenette, "a lot!"

So the three of us sat there in a row on the couch, we waved our USA flags and cheered as men and women in the peak of health and muscularity ran sprints and laps and hurdled hurdles and all of those track things we cared nothing about, but we cheered and waved our flags anyway.

The conversation with the Teacher kept coming back to me. I had never heard anyone question Federal Sam before, and it was like a switch was turned on. *If what they had done to the Teacher was wrong, and if Federal Sam lied to us, what was to say Federal Sam wasn't lying about other things? Or everything? And if that was the case…*

Back in the McVisa Olympic Studios, the hologram of Bob Costas interviewed the hologram of Muhammad Ali. Piano music played in the background. Ali talked about his childhood until he choked up, and a single tear descended to the champion's chiseled jaw line, which signaled that the interview was over.

We'd been drinking Federal Sam's Victory Black Lager, and we were a little drunk by the time it was over. Hope Jedia Smith, the night announcer for News Dispatch came on and delivered the evening news before dismissing USA members to "Carry on, the USA Way."

At eleven, the broadcast was over, and the News Dispatch announced that viewing was no longer compulsory for the evening, so we switched off the set.

But of course, it was never really *off*. Not completely.

I was wishing Tina would leave, and I think Laura could tell because she kept giving me this look whenever we were in the kitchen. But it wasn't her usual mischievous grin that she normally used to tease me into frustration. Something was wrong.

Tina was an insufferable gossip, and she and Lauren went on and on about people from their office. I didn't know most of the people they gossiped about.

"Tina, why don't you mix us some daiquiris?" Lauren said suddenly.

We all knew what that meant. Even the most loyal USA Members need the occasional private moment. The blender would drown out our voices while we spoke together.

"Oh yeah," Tina said. *"Daiquiris."*

Tina made the daiquiris and while she did, we spoke with our backs to the screen (even though it was off, it was common knowledge there were cameras active all the same).

With the blender going full blast, Lauren said, "I think we should see other people."

"What?"

She looked down and bit her lip. "I should be honest. I'm already seeing someone else."

"What?"

"I just thought—I just thought it would be easier for you to make your decision."

"Did they put you up to this?" She was lying. She had to be making it up.

"I'm sorry. I've changed my status to single."

* * *

The following morning, I went to meditation with the rest of the graduates. We sat facing the great painting of Federal Sam. White goateed, rosy cheeked, with a red, white and blue top hat, watery blue eyes, determined grimace, pointing out at us like an accusation.

PRODUCTIVITY.
OBEDIENCE.
VIGILANCE.

Of course, all I could think about was Lauren. It was over. She had made that clear. My head hurt from the drinks the night before. I wasn't hung over, but I had that thick, groggy feeling from staying up too late and having a couple of drinks.

I sat cross-legged and gave up any hope of meditation. I couldn't clear my thoughts; *I had too much to think about.*

Lauren was gone. She had filed with the F.S. Metabase that our relationship was over. I wouldn't be able to travel to her building anymore. I couldn't text or call her phone. I couldn't even contact her over the Internet. It was over. I was locked out. I had kept begging, and she had kept saying it was for the best. *For the best, for the best, for the best.* For the best what? She said I was most needed as a Teacher, and she didn't want to deny USA a qualified and talented Teacher.

I think she was just tired of me.

Or she was put up to it. F.S. had told her to end the relationship.

I kept telling myself that.

Either way, I knew now what I had to do. I would take the Red Robe and become a Teacher. I would be uploaded to the Metabase.

The north wing of the building was inaccessible now. I couldn't go back to speak to the Teacher who had warned me, and now I was beginning to think it was all just a trick, or a Teacher who had some unfounded complaint against Federal Sam. I would be uploaded, and that was that.

* * *

It wasn't what I had expected. They led me down a hallway, concrete blocks painted white. No windows. Tile floor, mottled brown. Our footsteps echoed: the F.S. Agents' boots, and my bare feet. There was no ceremony, no one there to congratulate me or say any speeches. Just a couple of F.S. Agents.

Had I known any better, I would have thought I was in some sort of trouble. I could sense the sneers behind the F.S. Agents' smiles. They weren't the usual thugs. They were big, but they looked somewhat educated. They spoke with less cruelty. They used longer words. Specialists of some kind. They still wore the powder-blue t-shirts, utility belts and khaki shorts.

"Does the upload take long?" I asked.

"What?" the agent on the left, the tall blonde said. "Oh, yes. The upload. It's done in a flash."

They opened the metal door and the tall blonde gave me a nudge, and suddenly I knew there would be no upload.

The metal cap.
Thick leather straps.
For wrist, ankles and chest.
Bound down to the thick wooden timbers.

"And I've been here thirty years," said the Teacher. "And 422S has been there longer than I have. And it's the same in all the other schools throughout USA, year after year after year. Where do you think all those graduates who choose to be uploaded really go?"

This was no upload. There were no data cables. Just thick electrical connectors, like on a car battery. This was no upload. This was an execution.

* * *

And in that instant, I went from Compliant USA Member to Non-Compliant Fugitive. Just like that. *In a flash.*

* * *

I lunged backward. They didn't expect it. Maybe no one had fought back before. Maybe no one had ever had a *warning* before. I pulled free of their grasp and I was sprinting down the hallway in my bare feet. I heard the Taser snapping, but they must have missed because then I was through the doorway and there were my shoes in the little bin and the guy behind the desk getting up too slowly, not sure what he was seeing. I grabbed my shoes mid-stride and barreled out into the sunshine.

Air-cars overhead, blasted air, white-bright sunlight. Downtown was blistering this time of day. I sprinted across the street to the downtown Freedom Mall.

"It's a lie! It's a lie! It's a lie!" I screamed through the Mall. All those graduates before me, so many of my friends, executed, not uploaded. F.S. was a lie.

I looked around and realized everything was a lie. Now I had announced it at the Mall. It was recorded. I was Non-Compliant. There would be no going back. I would have to head Out of Town. Out of Bounds.

F.S. Agents were on the move. I ran past the DiscoverCard-Chili's NASCAR Jalapeno-Poppers Experience Pavilion and out into the parking lot.

To the woods, to the woods, to the woods. I didn't even know where to run, but I made it.

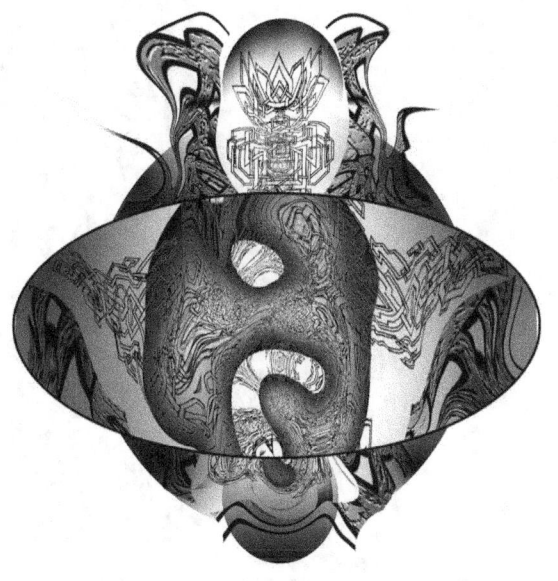

The Bridge is Out

We think we know
how we got here,
down that long dark highway.

We don't know
where we're going—
over a cliff?

— Neal Wilgus

Searching for King Arthur's Grave

Story by
Gary Every

Illustration by
Kathy Ferrell

I am searching for the grave of King Arthur on the autumnal equinox because once again Arthur's divine presence is needed. Enemies threaten to invade our island home. We need a resurrection of the once and future king, a battle-tested leader whose exploits make the angels sing. I stalk the forest at midnight searching the lunar glow for the ghost of a giant dog, intending to follow this behemoth canine wherever he goes.

On a windswept barren plain in the Welsh countryside I stumble upon the pile of rocks known as Carn Gafall. Carn is the Welsh word for any pile of stones meant to serve as a marker or monument but the one and only Gafall was once King Arthur's dog. I climb the massive monument of stone, hand over hand, rock by rock. Loose stones slip beneath my feet, cascading down the giant carn. With a grunt, I pull myself to the top of the giant pile of rock. The stone on the very top of that massive monument wears the track of a single dog paw. That dog print was left by Arthur's loyal hound Gafall who many centuries ago, while hunting for a wild boar, stepped on a stone a little too hard and left his paw print embedded in this rock forevermore. I steal this infamous stone, knowing that when darkness sets I will be able to use the paw print to follow the ghost of Gafall home.

The shadow of the giant dog appears at twilight, and then I hear the hound howling at the moon. Stone in hand I run as fast as I can while the ghost of Gafall galumphs through the forest. The huge canine stops to sniff everything in sight and pees on several trees. The night stretches on and on, still all Gafall does is sniff and pee, pee and sniff. I yawn and wonder if I will be forced to follow Gafall all night in order to find the grave of the greatest of all kings—Arthur or will I fall asleep before daybreak and awaken wondering if this was all a dream.

On the dark side of midnight, walking clumsily through the forest, I startle a large white stag. This beautiful deer leaps from its resting place, running at breakneck speed through the forest in darkness. Gafall takes up the chase, bursting through the underbrush leaving a wake of broken branches and leaves. The giant hound bays as he chases while the white stag runs and runs, magnificent beast gliding through the forest, rack of antlers rising from his head. As the buck leaps, ghost of a baying hound on his heels, the antlers grow and grow, through velvet and beyond, before dropping to the ground once more, then growing all over anew.

In the deepest hours of the night I am greeted by a wondrous sight. The white stag stops atop a hill—beautiful deer glowing in the moonlight. The magnificent beast turns his head branching antlers portrayed in crisp silhouette. The white stag leaps so high it seems to fly into the sky. Gafall gives up the chase, stopping to circle round and round sniffing a circle of stones upon the ground. The more Gafall circles and smells these stones upon the ground, the more I come to realize these stones are the ruins of a vanished prehistoric civilization. These large monoliths of rock, cracked and covered in vegetation, are laid out in a pattern, precisely measured, and carefully calibrated to mark an astronomical calendar. I was marveling at this prehistoric mathematical wonder when the earth begins to shake and quake, with a rumbling deep underground. Suddenly, giant stones are thrown into the air. Entire trees are uprooted and upended. The ground trembles as the soil fissures and a roar escapes from the underworld. I cower as the earth splits wider and a giant creature arises.

This beast is a bear, a behemoth of a bruin so much larger than any bear I have seen before. He is an extinct bear, a prehistoric monster who holds a sword in his hand. It is gleaming Excalibur.

I stammer a question, "A-A-Arthur?"

He nods.

"I was not expecting a bear," I said.

Arthur chuckles, his eyes twinkling like starlight. Then his powerful bear shoulders roll forward and grasping Excalibur's hilt with both paws he swings, felling the tree beside me, forcing me to leap from its falling path.

Arthur roars, mouth full of wind, fury and fang. "I am the original European," he explains. "We have been invaded by Normans, Norseman, Saxons, Christians, Celts, and Romans. We were overwhelmed by the Druids—Merlin's people, who built Stonehenge and Newgrange, refugees from Atlantis. Before history was invented there were Aryans and Indo Europeans, men with axes and chariots, who spread culture and languages as they conquered but still I survive."

It was the Roman generals who taught the historic King Arthur, a native war leader trained to defend the homeland after Hadrian's Wall had been abandoned. But the real Arthur, the once and future king, belongs to an older tradition dating back to the first humans to enter Europe, when men still battled saber toothed cats and Neanderthal for primacy. These original Europeans painted magical mysteries in caves in places like Las Caux, magnificent galleries of artful prayer. When these first men prayed, they prayed on altars made of cave bear bones, worshipping powerful prehistoric Pleistocene beasts. In the mountains of the Pyrenees, home of giant dogs like Gafall, there is one of these painted caves with an altar of cave bear bones collapsed in the corner and inscribed on the stone wall is the name of their bear god. They called him "Arcturus," the root of the word Arthur—the once and future king.

I explain how dire our present situation. How the great war leader is needed right now to defend our people, our island.

Arthur begins to laugh. How odd to see a bear laughing, belly shaking like a bowlful of jelly because no matter how jolly the bruin becomes you never forget his long claws or sharp fangs.

Then Arthur sighs and says, "The world situation is always desperate."

He grasps Excalibur like a javelin and throws it forward, straight and true. Arthur heaves Excalibur as hard as he can. The sword plunges into a boulder, blade quivering where it sticks.

As the dawn breaks and the sun rises, Arthur points to the sword and declares "Every generation must earn freedom anew."

Then he vanishes.

I stride to the boulder and with a great deal of effort pull the sword from the stone.

Properly mystically armed I stride into battle preparing to protect those I love and defend the most ancient of traditions.

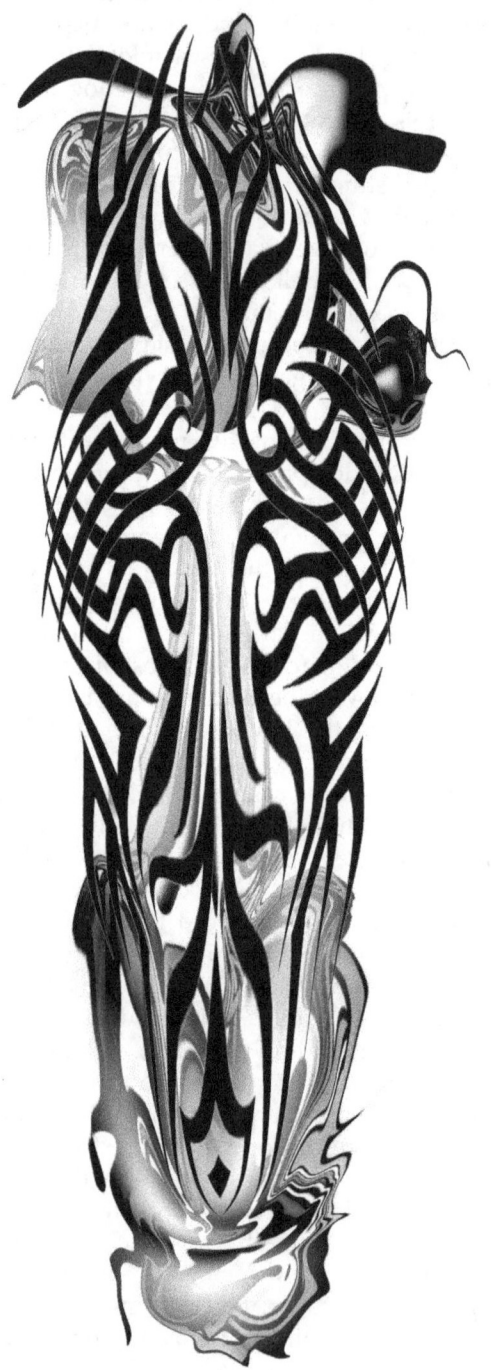

The Skip Tracer

The ice is still cold.
The glass still slightly sweaty
as condensation oozes and drips.
The seat is still warm.
The leather still slightly sweaty
as it reverts into shape.
The table is still damp.
The varnish still slightly sweaty
as hand prints and fingerprints disappear.
The candle is still warm.
The wax still slightly sweaty
as the flame flickers and
dies.

— L.B. Sedlacek

Behind the Walls

there is something there unseen
scratching and rustling behind the walls
buzzing that roots itself behind my eyes

It follows me it sometimes wanders
stalking something behind the walls
warded off by company but still heard distantly

they do not cease they do not relent
voices resolve from the noises behind the walls
murmuring chants that echo through the house

they now carry into my nightmares
sounds suggesting colors made behind the walls
twisting my perceptions to meet in alignment
with the Presence lurking behind the walls

— R. Donald James Gauvreau

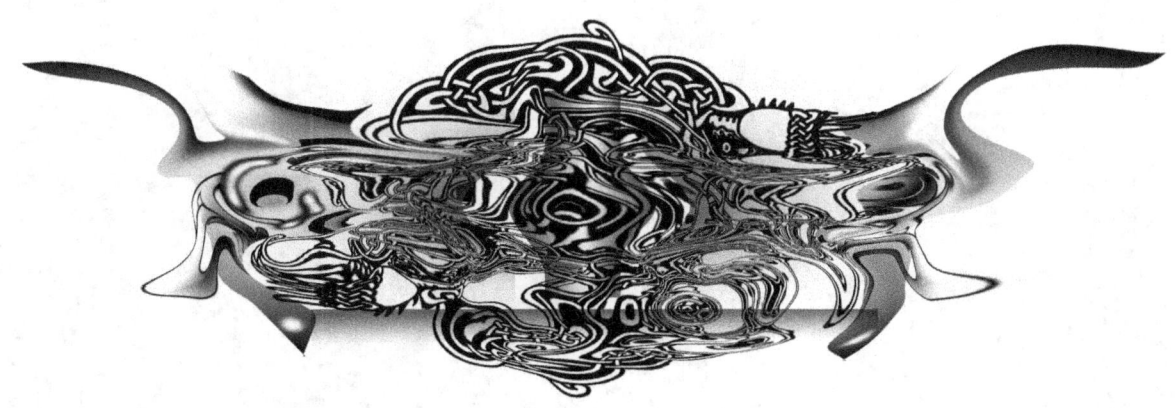

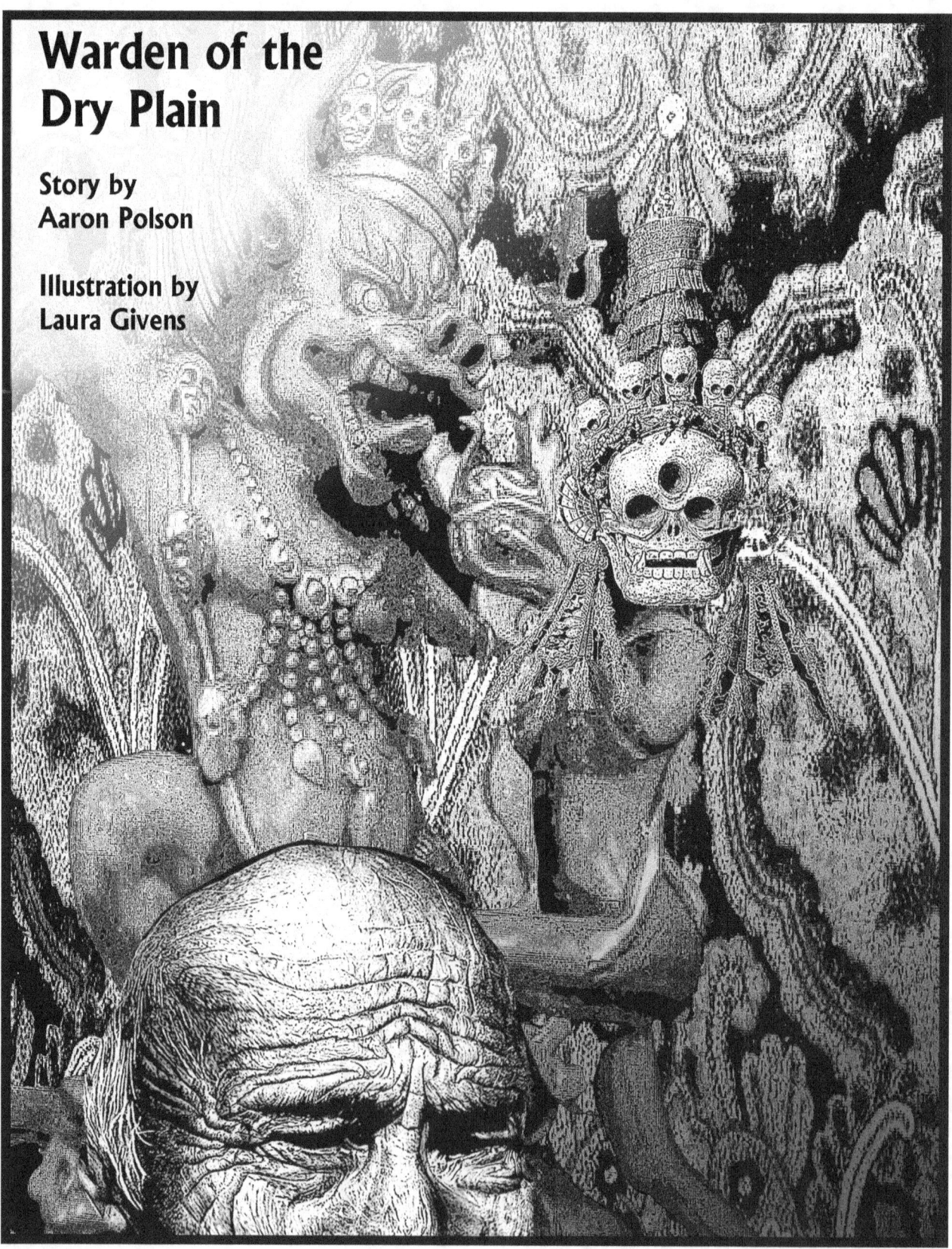

Warden of the Dry Plain

Story by
Aaron Polson

Illustration by
Laura Givens

Bataar glances at the American doctor, the tall one they call *stick-man* in Mongolian, as the truck bounces on a rocky path. Outside the window, the dry plain, an expanse of scrub grass and rock muted in grey-brown, stretches to the distant mountains. To Bataar it is only a job, not a calling and not an ancestral duty like the herders on the steppe with their yurts. The doctor has his list, his check sheet of roads to travel and families to visit; Bataar has the truck and a small wage and a clean apartment. It is a life.

The truck slows near a rounded tent which seems to have grown from the harsh ground.

"Is this it?" Dr. Stenner asks.

Bataar nods. He knows the yurt, his uncle's. He knew when he saw the doctor's checklist that morning.

The passenger door squeaks as Dr. Stenner opens it and hops to the ground. He pulls the fur-lined neck of his coat closer to his chin. Bataar watches from the driver's seat.

"Are you getting out?"

"Yes. Sorry." Bataar pulls his hands away from the wheel. He is not only the American's driver, but his translator as well. Uncle Chulunn has little English, and Bataar knows he's needed. His boots crunch the hard steppe ground. The wind bites his cheeks. "This is my uncle's place," he says.

Stenner looks up from his kit. "Uncle? Out here alone?"

"He likes it this way."

"Does he have family then—living with him, I mean."

Bataar shakes his head. "Not family."

"I see." Stenner rubs under his long nose with a gloved finger. "Why didn't you say something earlier? I'll be happy to meet your uncle." He offers a smile.

Bataar has come to accept Stenner's smile for what it is: awkward and out of place. The American doctor understands little of life on the steppe. He knows his role, hands out small first aid kits and pokes the children with inoculations, but he won't be part of Mongolia. He couldn't share history with Bataar and Chulunn and the rest of the children of the cold, harsh land. He won't understand the legends and myths like a native. Bataar's stomach turns to stone thinking of the monsters hanging in Chulunn's yurt.

"Well, let's make our visit then." Stenner strides toward the circular tent, pausing at the door flap. His eyes rest on Bataar, waiting for his translator to offer greeting.

Bataar nods. *"Uncle Chulunn? It is your nephew,*
Bataar. I am here with the doctor. He would like to speak with you."

A moment passes filled with no sound but the cold howl of wind across the earth. The steppe is kept clean by the wind, and it cleanses the people, too. Stenner shivers. Bataar's stomach of stone turns over. He can feel the eyes of the monsters. Perhaps his uncle will not answer, but then—

"Come in, please." The reply comes in English. Stenner smiles again and steps aside to allow Bataar first entrance.

If the choice was his, Bataar would never again enter his uncle's Yurt. The tapestries frightened him when he was a boy, and now, at twenty, he still carries a vestige of the fear. For as long as Bataar could remember, Uncle Chulunn covered the walls of his home with demons and strange creatures—red-eyed monsters and long human faces with teeth and tusks. Myths and legends, he had told Bataar.

Myths and legends.

"They watch you," Bataar had told his mother when he was a child.

"Nonsense," she'd said. "Nonsense."

Darkness hangs with the tapestries inside the yurt, and for a moment, Bataar is blind. As his eyesight returns, he finds his uncle, a shriveled relic, hunched on a cushion across the tent. Bataar nods to the old man. Chulunn offers a mouth filled with yellow teeth and black gaps.

"You look well, nephew. I've been worried since you haven't been to visit this old man in a long time. Too long."

"This is Dr. Stenner—from America. He wants to speak with you, check a few things."

Chulunn grunts. *"I've heard of the stick-man."*

Stenner steps forward and offers a hand to shake. Chulunn examines it like one might a herd animal for purchase and grasps it briefly. The doctor's eyes circle the interior of the yurt.

The walls are covered with tapestries, like any other yurt on the steppe, but these tapestries are different. Instead of bright designs and patterns, perhaps the occasional scene from a popular folktale, Chulunn's tapestries are filled with fangs and snarling lips, bulging yellow eyes, and claws. Monsters haunt the tent. Monsters from Bataar's childhood nightmares.

"You have interesting … decorations," Stenner says. He turns to Bataar and the two exchange a glance which, to Bataar, speaks to the strangeness of their surroundings. In the corner of his eye, Bataar sees a demonic mouth open in a grin. Claws flash across the yurt. The faint smell of sulfur finds his nose.

"If it's all right with you, Uncle, I think I'll wait with the truck. I want to check something under the hood before we make the trek back to the city." Bataar pulls his eyes away from Stenner and allows them to rest on his uncle.

"*Of course. The doctor and I won't be long. Be careful, boy.*"

Outside, the wind continues its mournful march over the harsh ground. Bataar feels the beat of blood through his body like the press of a giant's fingers around his chest. He stumbles toward the truck. The world is bright and quiet and simple outside. He leans against the side of the vehicle and allows cold air to come to his lungs. His ears wait, expecting something, the death-scream of the American doctor perhaps. To expect such things is folly, of course, as the hanging demons are but cloth and dye. Bataar knows this as well as he knows the navigation of the steppe without proper roads, but the childhood fragment of fear itches like an old splinter under the skin.

He closes his eyes as footfalls strike the hard ground.

"Ready?" Stenner asks.

Bataar turns and nods.

"Would you like to say goodbye? I can wait."

"No sir. Uncle will understand." Bataar's gaze falls on a black bundle under the doctor's arm. "What do you have?"

"Oh—your uncle wanted me to have one of his hangings. Strange things, really. I haven't seen any like them. I always like to collect an artifact or two from my travels. It helps me remember."

"Uncle gave it to you?"

"I didn't even ask."

Bataar's stomach grows cold. "We should go. Sunset will come soon."

"Yes, I suppose we should. Are you positive you don't want to say goodbye?"

Bataar shakes his head. "Uncle will understand. We haven't been close since I was a boy. We weren't close then. He's a different man."

"Oh?" Stenner pauses with a hand on the passenger door handle. "How so?"

"Just … different. He likes to be alone."

* * *

Bataar does not dream that night. He does not dream because sleep will not come. He lies awake on his mat, staring at the trim ceiling lines in his Soviet era apartment. Images of Dr. Stenner's face come to his waking brain, mixed with images of the smirking monsters in Chulunn's yurt. Why would uncle give away one of his tapestries? Bataar had never known him to do so.

Answers come to him, but none fit—not with his adult sensibilities. The child inside knows, though. The child understands what his uncle keeps locked in his yurt. The child remembers the stories his mother told about Uncle Chulunn's special job, how he was not a herder of animals but other things. It was a child's story, though—and it wouldn't explain why his uncle imparted a tapestry to the doctor.

It is this last puzzle which forces Bataar from bed before dawn. He dresses quickly and hurries down the stairs to the lot and his government truck. His imagination fills the holes in the puzzle with childhood fears, waking nightmares which will devour poor American Dr. Stenner. Folly, yes. Bataar knows he is foolish, but a night without sleep does little to aid rational thought.

At Dr. Stenner's house, Bataar kills the engine and climbs from the truck. The house isn't much. Stenner's organization—Doctors without Borders—pays the rent. Bataar stands at the door as the morning sun crests the horizon and spills icy shafts of light into the streets of Baganuur. His hand hesitates before knocking; he is early, perhaps too early and then he will need to explain his irrational fear to the doctor.

Bataar listens for a moment. Silence returns to him. In the silence, the beat of his heart swells and clogs his ears. His head fills with its throb, a constant, muffled *thump* which blocks the rest of the world. Bataar chews his lip. Knuckles rap against wood, *thud, thud, thud.*

"Dr. Stenner?"

No answer. He waits. Perhaps the doctor is still asleep. Perhaps his silly, night terrors are just that: foolish visions from Bataar's childhood. His neck and face warm with embarrassment. He should go, leave before the doctor opens the door and finds him standing, red-faced on the stoop. Then he will be forced to explain his nightmares and how Chuluun's tapestries frighten him like a baby. These thoughts mingle in Bataar's mind, but his feet do not move.

He knocks again because deep inside, beneath the thoughts of potential shame, he knows something is wrong.

"Dr. Stenner?"

Again, silence. Bataar tries the handle, and to his surprise, it moves. Darkness waits inside the house. Bataar steps back—the darkness is almost too much. Perhaps the doctor sleeps heavily.

But the door was unlocked. Surely…

He takes two steps inside the door and finds the smell, a faint hint of sulfur. Bataar wonders if his imagination conjures it, if the hours of lying awake and thinking the worst of Uncle Chuluun's motives have planted the odor in his mind. His eyes adjust to the darkness. His feet propel forward, into the small house. He remembers the floor plan from a visit to Dr. Stenner and makes for the American's bedroom. The quiet in the house nearly swallows him, nearly devours him and makes him part of it. Bataar holds his breath.

Certain shapes form in the darkness of Dr. Stenner's sleeping chamber: a small bed, a squat cabinet for clothing, a near-black object on the wall … the tapestry. Even in the dark room, Bataar can tell the bed is empty. His gaze shifts to the tapestry. His fingers find the light switch.

Bataar's mouth drops open in silent scream.

* * *

Bataar does not remember the drive to his Uncle's yurt. The trip takes nearly two hours, most of it over rough, untamed steppe ground, a drive requiring skill, but he does not remember the trip. His blood has become stone; his heart a dull chisel. He climbs from the truck with the black tapestry rolled in his arms. The cold wind plays with the cloth's edges. A tiny stream of smoke meanders from Chuluun's chimney. His uncle appears at the opening, a wry smile working on his lips.

How am I so lucky to have a second visit from my nephew?

"I've … I've come to return something," Bataar replies in English.

Chuluun ducks under the tent flap.

Bataar follows. His stony blood doesn't thaw under the yellow glares of two-score demons. The rolled tapestry grows heavy in his arms. He stumbles a few more steps and stops.

Chuluun stoops over his stove. "Tea?"

"No, Uncle. I … I…"

Chuluun turns. Shadows bend his face into a mock-demon. "Is it about the doctor?"

Bataar says nothing.

"I see you've returned my gift to him. Did it not please him?"

"Where did you learn English?"

Chuluun smiles. "From here and there. Why do you return my gift?"

The hanging demons tilt their heads, waiting for response. One drags its claws across the cloth slowly, a soft ripping sound. Bataar kneels on the nearest

cushion. His frozen hands thaw enough to unroll the tapestry. Instead of a demonic visage, the cloth now wears a sewn and dyed image of Dr. Stenner. Bataar has no words, in English or Mongolian, with which to describe the look on Stenner's face.

"Oh." Chuluun offers another wry smile. "I see. It seems your American friend has met his fate."

Bataar's fingers shake as he touches the image. "Fate? What have you done? He has vanished—this was left behind… What has happened to him?"

Chuluun brings a small cup full of steaming liquid to his lips. He nods. "He has been imprisoned, nephew. Trapped like the rest." The old man's eyes circle the interior of his yurt. "All of them, trapped."

"Trapped?"

"I am the guard and warden, Bataar. I have been my whole life."

"But Dr. Stenner … the image which was on his tapestry…"

"A decoy. I knew the American's soul when I met him yesterday. My duty, nephew, has always been to capture and keep the monsters."

"He was here to help."

Chuluun coughs and smiles again. "Help? He is just like all the rest. They want to banish demons with needles and their strict minds. They want the steppe to vanish and our yurts to crumble to dust. But they are demons, too, only of a different type."

Bataar shivers. "The rest?"

Chuluun sets his cup down and rises. He moves to a section of tapestries. Each demon's eyes follow him. Bataar is sure of it, no illusions now. The old man's hands pull a few hangings aside, revealing a second layer. From each black cloth, a human face peers out. The faces are frozen in looks of terror, but the eyes—like those of the monsters—move, shifting from Chuluun to Bataar.

"You wanted to know how I learned English? Your American wasn't the first, nephew. I've been collecting them for some time. Americans. Chinese. Europeans. Demons hiding in human skin. They only speak at night with the rest of the inmates, all of them—all the monsters—whispering to me while I sleep. You can't imagine the worlds I've known in dreams. The horrors."

"Uncle…"

Where would our world be without such prisons and those willing to guard them?

The Goat

Story by K.S. Hardy
Illustration by Laura Givens

I am the Goat.

Chosen, elected, and volunteered.

I know those words, if they seem to contradict each other or whose definitions appear to be exclusive of one another, may confuse those who in the future listen to this recording crystal but I assure that in my culture they have been by custom, grouped together.

Perhaps it would be best if I describe the ceremony of the Goat. The great tabulating computer kept in the kingdom's Department of the Census, normally used for the accounting of the queen's expenses and the assessing of the tax rolls, once a year is put to the task of randomly choosing from the entire population (excluding those of royal blood, of course) twelve nominees to be potentially, the Goat.

It is twelve, always twelve, the same as the number of apostles before Judas sought other employment.

Then the rest of the kingdom, after initialing the distributed broadsheets describing the candidates to certify that they had read them or in many cases, had them read to them, voted on who they wanted to become the Goat. Now here is one of the odder aspects of the tradition, the winner is the loser. Whoever receives the least votes, whoever is the most undesired, becomes the Goat.

But only if she or he volunteers. By decree and law, the Goat must accept the position by free will choice. It is the way. It is the understanding, for the service that the Goat provides, must be offered as a gift.

Here is how it comes about. The queen summons the loser to the castle and in the great hall before all of the royal court, it is she who descends from her throne and approaches the chosen one and then kneels before him or her, the only time the queen gets down on her knees for anyone except her gods, and begs them to volunteer on behalf of the people, to become the Goat.

And they always volunteer. For there is honor and yet dishonor attached to the position's name. And benefits.

Ah, this recording crystal is almost full, it is growing a darker shade of violet. The legend goes they were the making of an apprentice of Merlin's. Tiny jewels like cut diamonds, no bigger than a child's fingernail, that when you hold them to your lips and speak into them they memorize your voice. Then when you wish to hear what they contain, you hold them to your ear and gently rub the gem with your fingertips and all is recounted for your listening pleasure. As I said they begin clear as diamonds but change color as they fill, first to the green of emerald, then the blue of sapphire, turning red as ruby as warning of almost being full, and then black as coal when the crystal's recording is completed. Mine were given to me by a scribe from the royal scriptorium who has the strange notion to produce a volume of the daily Life of the Goat.

* * *

Here begins the second crystal. My apologies, I was thus instructed to do that by the scribe, so he could keep them in order.

Where was I?

The benefits. The honor and dishonor. There are no direct benefits for the Goat. But for the Goat's family, father and mother if they are still be alive, the spouse and offspring, there accrues much.

They are adopted by the queen, with all it entails except for the line of succession. This is how her royal court has become so large. The richest of foods, the finest of clothes, and any instruction in the arts desired, from embroidery of tapestry to the diplomacy of courtly intrigue to writing of haiku verse. And this does not last for only the year of the Goat's tenure, but for each family member, it is a lifelong blessing.

So who would not volunteer to be the Goat to insure the welfare of their family?

And the honor. Think of it. The queen, the most powerful person of the realm, commander of armies and fleets, who can behead at will or send out zeppelins on world-circumnavigating journeys bowing at your feet.

She did to mine.

Then, after I had acquiesced to the queen's request, she backed slowly away as prescribed by ritual. Six of her knights stepped forward, disrobed me, and then I was offered a chair of gold. This was placed on a litter which they lifted up upon their shoulders. I was then paraded around the great hall to the dainty applause of the court, then out through the brass doors into the palace grounds, and then beneath the portcullis into the city beyond the castle walls where the populace, a massive crowd that assembled every year for this was the celebration of the year, cheered me with enthusiastic "huzzahs".

Thus I was transported up and down the cobblestone streets for all to gaze upon.

For all to view my nakedness.

For did not I also say there was dishonor. This was only a small foretaste of it.

Finally I was carried to the Ezekial round about, a great circle in the center of the city where all the main roads did converge that in theory was to facilitate the flow of the carts and carriages. But here was what had been named, the Goat's Cage, was located.

It was a case and not a cage. It was a glass enclosure, transparent on all sides for all to see what was held within. It was four meters in height, about six meters in space, and hexagonal in shape, suspended from a golden chain.

Within was the one I was to replace, a woman, still as naked as the day she had been inducted. I was required to wait as they performed the ceremony of dismissal which I will not describe at this time, better to save that for my own dismissal.

* * *

This is crystal number three. I am to recount in detail my days for the scribe. His idea is to have a testament of a Goat's life to better study the spiritual benefits my service bestows upon the people.

After the dismissal of my predecessor which involved the shattering of one glass panel with an ivory mallet, I was installed. A new panel was attached, the seams secured by fusing the glass with a blow torch.

This, my first day, I was left alone. A rule observed so that the Goat can become accustomed to its surroundings. Therefore I will describe my cage. As I have said it is made of glass, with a glass ceiling and floor. No furniture. I sleep on that hard floor. Air holes in the top. More holes, two to a side near the bottom of each panel. They serve two purposes, the top for better circulation and the bottom, to sluice my waste out once a week with a hose as there is no place to defecate.

And there is no privacy. Remember, all is glass. Privacy for the Goat is not an attribute of the Goat.

And I am still naked.

There is I might add, in one panel, a small door, only large enough to allow for my daily delivery of food.

There is no escape. The glass is thick enough that only the mallet, large enough that it takes two knights to swing, can shatter it.

There is no leaving.

My new home is suspended by a chain fixed to a wrought iron armature that is very baroque in design. This beam extends over a small staircase of like metal that rises from the pavement to a cabinet wherein those who seek an audience with the Goat can sit. They do have privacy. The cabinet walls secure them from the view of the passer-by on the roundabout. And a red velvet curtain may be drawn to hide them from my view if they so desire. Although, in reality,

this is a false sense of privacy, for anyone can observe who comes and goes up the staircase. They do get to sit on velvet cushions.

I have no such comfort. Not a bed or a quilt to sleep on. Only glass. But what of my discomfort? As a farm laborer I did not have much before. Now I have a meal every day, and a copious one at that, for I must survive the required year. It would not do to starve the Goat. My comfort, a sacrifice I willingly made to better provide for my family. My wife, I imagine in silk dresses. My son being schooled by the finest tutors. My daughter perhaps learning painting or cross stitch. And they are well fed and cared for. What more can a head of the family ask?

* * *

Crystal number four.

People have started to come.

It seems that no one wanted to be the first.

And the first was a small boy. He broke the ice. He looked so innocent. In his nervousness, he forgot to draw the curtain.

"I bring you my sin," he said following seating himself on the cushioned bench.

I assumed the ritual position. Kneeling before the deliverer, buttocks resting on heels, arms outstretched at right angles to my shoulders as if to embrace the visitor, my eyes closed.

"I am ready to take on your burden."

"I steal."

Then the boy confessed. Money from his mother's purse. Candy from the corner bodega.

I received. I accepted.

And the boy left with a smile on his face.

As soon as the boy had left I heard a delicate, measured footfall on the steps.

(From here on the content of the fourth crystal had been mysteriously deleted, editor.)

* * *

Excerpt from crystal ten.

I have just received from a middle aged man a disturbing sin.

He fantasizes about killing his wife. Strangling her in her sleep. Poison in her tea. Stabbing her with her very own crochet needles.

He drew the curtain. The fool, does he not realize I clearly saw his face before he pulled it across I could easily identify him to the palace guard. He is of the court.

I can only hope that unburdening to me has relieved some of the homicidal pressure building up in him.

If he returns, I will report him.

* * *

Crystal twenty-eight.

They did not tell me about the dreams. Every confession. Every sin. Replayed each night like a recording crystal in my mind.

The thefts. The wished-for murders. The covetousness. The envies. The lusts.

I find it difficult to sleep. I close my eyes every night with dread.

* * *

Crystal thirty-three.

I cannot see out of my cage. Those passing by spit at the hexagon, for they believe that it will bring them favor from the Fates. My view is blurred by the spittle.

* * *

Crystal fifty-nine.

Today my daughter came.

I thought at first to visit, although that is frowned upon by the authorities.

No, she had a sin.

Her sin is that she wishes her father was dead. Because of the shame he has brought her.

There is dishonor as well as honor.

I wept.

* * *

Crystal sixty-three.

The sins are becoming more than I can bear. They weigh me down.

Today was a sluicing day. When they come with the water cart, a tank on a wagon that has handles on either side to pump up the pressure. A hose is inserted through my feeding door and the waste sprayed away. I stood deliberately in the direct gush of the stream, hoping to wash the sin away also.

It did not work.

Now I have added bruises to my suffering.

* * *

Crystal two hundred, I think.

I have lost track of the days.

And of the crystal count.

The scribe comes to take them away, bringing more with each visit.

I say that I am sorry. That I know that perhaps I am negligent in regards to my assignment for him.

He, the scribe, says he understands. That this in itself, tells much about the plight of a Goat.

* * *

The last crystal.

This one I hid. Where, I best not tell.

Yesterday I was dismissed.

I was almost joyful when they smashed the glass.

But what followed, quickly removed that joy. Erased it all.

Rotten fruit was hurled at me. Brown squishy apples. Putrid oranges grown black with mold. Everyone gathered in the roundabout had come well-armed with some sort of missile.

This is tradition.

And I am grateful.

In the olden days the Goat was driven from the city with stones, often resulting in death.

Perhaps, it might have been better.

But someone with wisdom pointed out that a dead Goat sort of defeated the whole purpose of the year-long rite.

I have now my freedom. And yet, do not have my freedom. The sins, all the sins given to me so that the giver might be sinless, they are still with me.

No one told me that I would not be able to shed them.

The dreams. The dreams are also still with me.

I have been driven into the wilderness and I wander. The dreams. They weigh my heart. They eat my soul.

They haunt me.

An Elephant in the Living Room

Story by
Christine Marie Angela

Illustration by
Laura Givens

Cathelos drummed his calloused fingertips on the shiny wooden coffee table that divided his living room couches. It was Saturday night, and guests would be arriving soon. Sighing, he conjured images of yet another dull evening with the same people coming over, the same conversation, the same wine and food.

Realizing that another night like this might claim his sanity once and for all, he stepped into his bedroom and closed the blinds. Kneeling down on the floor, he peeled back the carpet from under the dresser, and then he peeled back the floor itself.

And then he peeled back the World, and he climbed down into the abyss that was under the World.

He rummaged for some time. Finally, he found what he sought.

Re-emerging with a small elephant, Cathelos led the beast into his living room. Its wrinkly hide was grayish and careworn. It was not fully grown, but took up most of the available space that wasn't consumed with couches and chairs. Smiling for the first time in weeks, Cathelos began pouring glasses of wine, setting cheese blocks on trays, and waited for the guests to arrive.

When the bell rang, he greeted them with uncommon cheer. He ushered them in, taking their coats with glee, and zestfully zipping around them as they settled, passing out plates and food with the eagerness of a first time host. As the guests assembled in the living room, they chattered the usual commentary about the atrocious weather, the sick child at home, the frustrating job, the contemptuous news item of the week.

Cathelos waited until the room had settled, and then looked eagerly at his guests, awaiting their shocked response. But nothing happened.

Then, Matthias said, "Friend! Your home is always so warm and welcoming. Yet I sense a change." The others nodded and murmured in mild conjecture.

The trunked gray beast in the room snorted but no one turned towards it. Cathelos waited, still hopeful.

"It's the walls," said Jezebel. "You've painted them." The others mused their mutual agreement. Heads nodded, and wine glasses were sipped casually. When Cathelos did not confirm, another voice spoke.

"It's not the walls, you idiot. He's changed his hair. Gone a little shorter, have you? And the beard, is that new as well?"

Cathelos sighed, but barely had time to experience his frustration as the bell rang again.

It was an unexpected guest. How delightful! A neighbor with whom he barely spoke, but had often admired from afar. Her head was down, and her long dark hair concealed what he knew were strikingly beautiful violet eyes. She'd arrived on his doorstep entirely uninvited, which he found quite … inviting.

"Please," he said. "Come inside. It's cold. I have some friends over, and you are more than welcome to join us."

She did not speak but crossed the threshold gratefully, her eyes meeting his, and discarded her coat in his arms. She entered the elephant-consumed living room and found a seat. The group was still commentating on what remodeling Cathelos may have done to cause the felt change. Some said it must be new furniture; others were sure their host had lost weight.

The new arrival joined the conversation. Her voice was low and musical. "You mean, this elephant was always here? I cannot imagine that, since I live nearby, and have never seen the droppings."

Cathelos smiled warmly at her, and waited for the others to notice. But they did not.

"What elephant?" said Matthias. "Are you mad, or joking?" The others were frowning at her.

She raised an eyebrow at Cathelos but did not immediately respond. Finally she said, "Well I know I am not joking, and I may be crazy for sure, but still, there is an elephant in this room."

A pause ensued, not unlike the pause that occurs when a server stumbles and breaks a dish, and the entire restaurant freezes and feels pity for the dish-breaker, while simultaneously experiencing relief that it wasn't them causing the commotion.

The group felt embarrassed for this new lady, whom they assumed was crazy. Finally someone awkwardly changed the subject back to discussion of local events, sports news, and the usual boring banter.

Cathelos yawned. After a few hours of non-noticement of the elephant, the group began to dissipate. Once they'd all left but the neighbor, Cathelos turned to her.

"So … you can see the elephant?" he said.

"I don't really understand how he could be missed," she said, in amusement. "How often does one have an elephant hanging out in the middle of the living room?"

Cathelos smiled.

His friends, it seemed, were so used to the ordinary, that when the extraordinary presented itself, not only were they resistant to opening their minds to strange possibilities, they were unable to see it altogether.

But this girl was different.

"What are you doing next Saturday night?" he asked. "It seems I may need to change my original plans."

Their eyes met. And she did not speak, but smiled at him.

Strawberry Milkshake

Take Joe, for instance.
Never did give a damn
about exercise,
but then, that's why
they chose him,
pre-fattened for the pot—
huge, smelly thing
at city central, all cities
planet-wide now
we hear.

We don't go out
anymore. That's when
they take you—
snouts snuffling
like grotesque elephant trunks
dangling down
from their spacecraft,
slithering along streets,
sniffing like cadaver dogs,
encoiling the unlucky,
and crushing them,
boa-style,
to boil in the pot—
dissolving, liquefying,
then cooling
to get sucked up
like a strawberry milkshake.

Can't help but
imagine what lives
at the business end
of those stinking,
sucking snouts.
Terrified I might
eventually "see" one
from the inside.

— Lauren McBride

To See If It Is Possible

Story by
Erin K. Wagner

Illustration by
Morland Gonsoulin

May 1931.

Went to bed early dreamed of a demon with eyes four hundred feet apart

—Thomas Edison

He often wandered out onto the porch when it was still dark, when there was not yet a warning of dawn, when Mina still slept—seemingly soundly—often he found that he wanted to reach a hand out and shake her roughly, as if to assure himself that she was not Mary and that she was not in a sleep nearer death, induced by morphine. He lit a cigar and let it hang heavy on his lip, the ember dancing at the corner of his eye. He watched the street through the smoke. There were trees here, on his road. The wind brushed through them sometimes and he could hear this at night, when the rough noises of motors were few and far between. He had not shaken Mina. He had let her be. His fingers trembled as he took the cigar from his mouth and rested his hand on the arm of the rocking chair, his fourth and fifth finger tapping on the wood. Tapping, this fidget was a pattern and a habit.

Sometimes, he did not recognize his own body. In his head, he and his body were uneasy allies. They had worked in sync once, energy and flesh and invention together, but now. He rocked in the chair and felt his feet press the boards of the porch through his thin-soled shoes. Now, the pain in his stomach and the belly that strained at his waistcoat seemed to be setting their own pace, one much slower, much more labored than his mind. He was dressed fully, because he did not intend to return to bed. And in the hour of dawn, for which he waited, eyes turning every so often to the eastern horizon, he knew he would find a thought as translucent as the early spring leaves against the new sun, a thought that burned on bamboo fibers, leaving behind only fine charcoal dust to fade invisible into light. He closed his eyes. He could taste the smoke at the back of his throat. "Bad. It's bad," he said. He dropped the cigar and crushed the end with his foot.

He was still in the chair. He slipped his watch from his pocket and found that he could see the face of it. The sky grew lighter. It was this gloom, poised to brighten, that reminded him of his home as a boy. He watched his mother move from lamp to lamp in the dim light of early morning, hearing her dress swish against her leg and whisper against the floor. The pale skin of her hand glowed white next to the glass globes of the lamp as she reached a long match to light the wick and as she turned, with a practiced lack of thought, the knob at the neck of the brass base. He sat near the window and watched the world outside grow darker in contrast to the light inside. "Eat, Tom," his mother said, and put a bowl of warm cereal in front of him. He let his breakfast grow cold. When she told him again, he pretended that he had not heard her the first time. She believed this. The scarlet fever of the year before made her believe this.

Someone he had told, more than twenty years ago, believed that the rough handling of a train porter had deafened him. The man had hit him up the side of the head, he had told this forgotten stranger, stranger because forgotten. He raised his head, and realized his chin had fallen to his chest. He was glad he had dropped the cigar before. He had not missed the sunrise. He waited for the idea to come. They came to him now, in the moment between dark and light, sitting before the window with the room reflected behind him, sitting on the porch with the birds starting to rustle and trill. He was not, as other men thought him, a pragmatist. In the evening, with the last sun cutting through the windows of his study, he read poetry. He thought, in some way, that his own work was like the fragmented, unpunctuated thought of the poets he read. In his lab, his work was a run-on sentence, without comma or stop. This was because he had built it up around him and there was no one to stop him. "There is no shame in being proud of work well done," he had told Teddy when he was the age that he himself had started in the telegraph office. He translated the message into Morse without thought, because the age had reminded him and his son's face had reminded him. There had been those who accused him of having no ideas he could claim his own. There had been those who accused him of cruelty. Of opportunism. And of falsehood. "I do my work well," he said to Henry when he asked about one newspaper article. "And for that, I am proud." He had peddled newspapers once to passengers disembarking from trains, and he had done that well too.

The new sun was hitting the lattice of the porch, splitting into rays, and marking lines of shadow on the wood. His stomach had settled. He was convinced the cigar aggravated his dyspepsia. "Stop smoking, then," Mina said. "I can't, love. The taste is a stimulation to my mind. I can feel it working as I do." He waited for the idea. Like the glass shards in a kaleidoscope spinning and settling into crystal patterns, he felt his mind rattling, seeking a resting place. There was the rumbling of a truck engine in a near alley. Glass bottles rattled as a premonition of some coming milkman.

The dawn had come and darkness gone. A newspaper thumped at his feet and the paperboy screamed some unheard greeting.

He stood up, the chair creaking and rocking back behind him. Leaving the butt of the cigar where it lay but taking the newspaper, he walked through to the kitchen. The maid had not yet come, so the room was empty. He opened the refrigerator. There were eggs and vegetables crowded together and a glass bottle, half-empty, of milk. He took the bottle and a mug from the cupboard and moved into the sitting room. This room was still dim, designed to catch afternoon light. He waited here for Teddy to arrive with the car. The newspaper he spread out across his lap, but did not read. He drank the milk slowly. In the corner of the room, a covered cage swung slightly. The parrot was stirring, but he made no noise. He could make no noise. He was a bird that defied convention, deaf and dumb. "We two," he said and thought how no one would see him here if they passed, with the lights turned off—he missed the ritual of the lamps, "We two, we cannot hear."

"And what idea do you have today?" Teddy asked as the car idled in the driveway. He spoke differently now than he had even ten years ago. His tone had lost some subtle tone, a modulation of deference.

"You'll know when you need to," he answered.

The top was down and the motor was loud. The houses clicked by like images in the window of a train. Teddy parked at the sidewalk before the labs and the silence was loud. Menlo Park bragged of trees on the corners and casual strollers, imitating parks it had seen, but he saw only the shelves upon shelves of collected materials, the work desks and the burn marks, the crackles and the tapping that the fronts of the buildings hid. Stone, respectable, and glass to see through, to cast competing light onto the floors.

"Remember, the newspaper is coming for an interview today." Teddy lifted his hat and re-settled it on his head.

He nodded. Here was the cave of wonders, and the reporters whispered *open sesame* often. He felt a hollow ache behind his eyes, an emptiness pressing into the sockets. Though he stood beside him, Teddy seemed distant. "They will get a story," he smiled. He gestured his son ahead, and followed behind him, relief settling over him as he stepped in under the lintel and patted the doorframe with an appearance of bonhomie. The secretary took his hat and reminded him again of the reporters. "And Mr. Ford has sent over a blueprint." He nodded. He moved to his desk and stared at the items spread on it in a calculated mess. A small pair of scissors and a spool of metal wire, and a schematic for an engine that Henry had sent over for his review. And a straight key from a telegraph office, disconnected, but still useful for occupying his fingers when he looked over sketches and blueprints. That had largely been how the task had functioned in his days as an operator as well. Ideas ticked out in dots and dashes, while the messages translated through him were relayed without thought.

"And do you believe such a thing is possible, Mr. Edison?" The reporter had leaned forward towards him eagerly as if proximity would yield an answer more easily headline worthy. He had felt then as he did now. At a lack, with all the tools he could desire mocking him. The turn of conversation had been a strange one, but precipitated by his own comments. He had answered in a steady voice. It was important that one believed in the moment what one said. Sometimes they trusted you then. "I have been at work for some time building an apparatus to see if it is possible for personalities which have left this earth to communicate with us." He had later disclaimed it as a joke. In the back of his mind, though, he had remembered the séance his mother had once held in the living room. He sat in the corner, looking at the women huddled around the table. His mother had covered the table with a lace cloth, but he knew it was where they ate their breakfasts and dinner, earthly and mundane. The murmur of the medium sounded faint to his ears. They were using candles instead of the lamps. "Mrs. Kalewski asked it of me, Tom. She said it was all the rage. But I feel bad about it now. My father would have scolded me, Tom. He would have been very angry. He would have quoted Samuel to me—*I saw gods ascending out of the earth.* The witch of Endor said that. Tom, it was a foolish thing. We're not meant to lay eyes on God. Not in this form." She spoke rapidly, trying to hide her actual concern behind quick words, her tongue tripping and clicking.

He sat forward and pressed down the tongue on the straight key, holding it before letting it go. A sound that meant nothing, neither dot nor dash. "A language even those without tongues could utter," he muttered.

June 1931.
somewhere i have never travelled, gladly beyond
any experience, your eyes have their silence:

in your most frail gesture are things which enclose me,
or which i cannot touch because they are too near
                                        —e.e. cummings

He waited for Mina to go to bed before working at night. She hated to see him so preoccupied as they talked, though her own fingers teetered up and back over knitting needles. The evening had encroached early, his thoughts still winding through this new idea, looking at it from all angles. They sat across from each other in the sitting room, the parrot glaring down at them solemnly. Mina insisted that the bird was not angry, but he was not sure. "What would it do without us?" she said, and he thought perhaps it might do many things, in some humid jungle where the leaves dripped green and the air pressed hard on your lungs. He looked at Mina, her hair glowing whiter than it actually was in the light of the electric bulb. She was old now, and so was he. Mary had been so young, and she would be young forever.

"Teddy said the newspaper was at the lab again today," she said. The needles ticked and tapped against each other, long and short.

He nodded.

"What more have you got to say?" She smiled to herself and paused a moment, using her hand to smooth down the blanket or quilt or cozy that she was busy over. "What more do they want from you?"

He tapped a message on the arm of the chair, his finger lingering just a hair longer on the cushion for a dash.

"Everything and nothing, Tom?" She set the needles back at each other, looping one strand of yarn around the needle she held still.

"You still remember?"

She looked at him. Her forehead wrinkled slightly and she put the knitting down. She placed her hand trembling against her cheek as if feeling for something.

"Would I forget, Tom?"

He remembered her, a girl of twenty, with glossy hair and soft, downy wrists. They were seated in the back of someone's car, and she was close to him. She smelled like salt-water and melted sugar—candy left too long in the sun. He had been convinced that their ages, despite any calendar, were the same. He was young and she was old, and they were the same. When she had asked, the catch in her voice that exhibited when she was nervous, to be taught Morse, he had known he would propose to her. In the back seat, so the driver would not hear, he tapped his offer against her wrist.

"No," he said.

She folded the blanket and slid it under the lid of her sewing basket. She stood, and with shuffling step, went to the parrot's cage and pulled the cloth over the bars.

"Goodnight," she said.

He stayed up, late into the night, thinking over the plans he had sketched out. He remembered most of it, could even feel the rough paper under his hand where he had held it still under his pencil. He calculated for temperature and corresponding air pressure. The tongue would have to work on a hair trigger. Perhaps a box to shelter the thin wires.

The room was dark. He hefted himself from his chair with his arms stretched out behind him. The chair creaked. The bird shifted under his sheltering cloth, but made no other noise. "Quiet?" He laughed to himself. The laugh cut into his chest, sharper than a cough.

Mary had laughed so much when he first met her, sixteen years when they married. It was so near death, her sleeps, he had thought. The doctors had said the morphine was necessary, though, the only thing that kept her calm. It was something in her brain, they said. He watched her in the day and in the morning when she blinked her eyes slowly and wandered from the sitting room to the kitchen. Perhaps a tumor. "Mary." Sometimes she turned to look at him. Sometimes she did not hear him.

"The brain is electrical," he had told her once, sitting at the bedside, staring absently at the sunlight outside the window. "Why should it stop working because our organic flesh has?" He glanced at her. She was lying very still. Her face was pale, the skin almost translucent so that she glowed faintly in the brightness. She was calm. "We're all flesh," she said. Her voice was a drawn out whisper. "All of us flesh, I mean." She shook her head. "Every part of us," she tried to clarify. He put a hand on her arm and she stopped struggling to speak. "I know what you're saying, Mary." And her laugh was low and hoarse and seemed brittle inside her.

He left the sitting room and went to the kitchen. He opened the refrigerator and found there the same things as always. Vegetables, eggs. And here and there a new thing. A leg of lamb wrapped in brown paper and labeled in the butcher's rough scrawl. Two glass bottles of milk, one full, and one nearly full. He took the one bottle and poured himself a cup. He drank the milk, leaning back against the island counter. The fat lingered on his tongue. He had the feeling that he sometimes did that if he turned at just the right moment, across the doorway of the kitchen, Mary would pass, her white gown clinging to her legs. "A ghostly bigamist," but that had not been quite what he meant to say.

In the basement, down a narrow and unstable set of stairs, he kept a small desk with a few tools. He clicked on the electric light and went down.

July 1931.

It would have been more logical if silent pictures had grown out of the talkies instead of the other way round.
—Mary Pickford

When he was young, he had worked in a telegraph office. He worked the night shift and it suited him. The street outside was dark, and the lights at the front of the office dim, so that he could hardly make out the writing reversed on the window. He saw instead his own reflection, in two layers of glass. Sitting behind the counter, with a pane of glass between him and the front office. At his hand, he had a pile of slips with the Western Union logo. He held the pencil in his fingers most of the time, even if not writing. What few noises came from the street outside he could not hear well. And then, occasionally, a clattering message. These he always heard. Disembodied voices, mute tongues straining against the inside of the mouth. Men sick, women dying, children born. These were often the messages at night, bouncing along the wires, like the reflection of light on metal, skipping, transient.

He sat at the desk in his basement. The floor beneath his feet was packed dirt. There was a crate beside his chair, opened, the lid flung beside in his haste. He lifted the box out with both hands, settling it gently before him. A piece rattled inside it, but this was not a message, but rather the random trembling noise of something out of place. The box was constructed of the thinnest metal and the top opened on spiraled wire hinges. He opened the top panel and moved the box slightly so that it was centered under the bulb. With one finger, he reached in, careful to touch nothing else, and reattached the thin loop of wire around the screw from which it had disattached.

He left the top panel open and leaned back in the chair. He felt tired. He had brought from the office as well the straight key and he set it now beside the box. Then, he stood, hesitating a moment, and took from a shelf on the closest wall a wax candle. He lit the candle and stood it in an old dish, rusting. Then he clicked off the light. The flame of the candle flickered in the breeze of his movement, then licked high as he sat down and was still. The flame settled. Shadows flickered on the wall.

He waited quiet. The box worked, he supposed, on the assumption that the spirits wished to speak. That for him, someone waited just beyond a thin wisp of curtain that could be pushed aside with a breath. He thought that it would not be his mother who talked. She had disapproved of spirits and séances, and though he knew this to be strange reasoning, he felt assured of it. He knew who he thought it must be.

He did not love Mary more than Mina. It had occurred to him that an outside observer would be moved to this conclusion if they could trace his thought and his anticipation. He imagined, though, that no reporter would ever know this, this silent waiting, this unknown hope. When he turned his understanding on himself, he felt that hollowness, that empty ache. Mina had learned Morse, had looked over his schematics with eager interest if not total comprehension. She knew before he did the onset of his stomach pains. She carried Tulu gum with her at all times in case he would need it. And behind the laughter, what had Mary said? What had she known? He could hardly remember her speaking now at this distance. All of us flesh, she had said, and this he did not believe.

There was a heaviness of silence in the room, the house above pressing down. "Well, Mary, what have you to say?" He thought, perhaps, some concession to usual practice might be necessary. He addressed the spirit.

The candle burned down as he waited, and when it was snuffed out by its own absence, he did not light another, but remained sitting in the dark. He could feel the desk in front of him, and for this experiment, vision was hardly necessary. It was a just a voice that he desired to hear, translated through dots and dashes. He worked out on the straight key, though it was not wired to anything, his question again. The tapping sounded small and quiet, muted by the darkness.

Eventually, the door at the top of the stairs creaked open and Mina's voice came, concerned. She was asking for him, and he could see the light of day from the open door. Here he had waited the night, and though he saw no scientific reason why the spirits would only speak at night, he knew his experiment was over. He stood up, the chair scraping in the dust. He turned on the electric light. The box and the wires within in it mocked the light that shone on it. He saw, in front of him, a crude instrument without intellectual refinement, without a spark of genius. It was simpler even than the telgraphs he had operated as a young man.

He felt moved to grab it up and throw it violently at the further wall, a desire to see the thin metal bent and the wires tangled beyond repair. But he closed the top panel and he left it there on the desk. He went upstairs into the daylight.

October 1931.

Promise to give me a kiss on my brow when I am dead. I shall feel it.

—Victor Hugo

He lay silently after Mina left. She had been reluctant to go, as if to miss the transition from life loosely held to life gone were a matter of any moment. He was too weak to move his own legs, and this seemed a death as sure as any other. Soon, his children would arrive, and they would want to crowd in and take one last look and this is what they wished to preserve in their memory: an old man unsure of his own movements. He flung his arm with force in order to shift it and so that it hung over the side of the bed. His fingers searched, clawing at the air. Then he found it, the thin metal box that he had shoved just under the end of the quilt. He had moved it here a week ago or less. Left in the basement, it had been cold to the touch when he had picked it up. It felt right to have the box near him, though, as if—for some inexplicable reason—it might talk and no one would be there to hear. Now that he was confined to his bed, he felt the silence of the box as strongly as any companion, wife or child or friend. To have anyone else in the room felt crowded and the air seemed to grow stale.

The door opened slowly as if the person behind feared to let in a draft. "Hurry in, if you're coming," he barked. Charlie edged his way in and paused at the door as if hesitant to step too close.

"It's not catching."

"I know that, Da," his son's voice was ashamed. His face was very pale and he looked as if he had something unpleasant on his tongue.

"Teddy here too?"

Charlie nodded. "And all the rest of us. Maddy, Will, Tom and Mary."

"Dot and Dash," he said. Charlie smiled slightly. "But you're not kids anymore."

"Not for a long time," Charlie said.

"Should I say Tom and Marion, then?"

"It doesn't matter. You can call us whatever you want."

He shifted as best he could on the mattress, seeking a different cotton hollow for his body.

"It matters now as much as it ever will, Charles. My brain's not gone, even if my body won't answer to it."

Charlie stepped forward. He placed a small glass vial on the bedstand. It was empty.

"What's that?"

His son moved back again, his hands thrust in his pockets.

"Mr. Ford asked me to bring it in. Thought you might fancy something of you remaining after."

He tried to reach for the vial, but his fingers merely grazed the bamboo edge of the table.

"And what part of me am I to leave behind?"

Charlie shifted his weight from one foot to the other. "He said for me to get some of the air of the room. To save your last breath, he said."

He felt the air in his lungs and the pressure there, a hollow empty pressure, without substance but there nonetheless. "Breath of God in us," he said and he remembered his mother's voice, but the sound was mingled with the vision of lamp-light flickering and the smell of logs cracking in the stove. There was no individuality to the senses of his memory. He smelled the piercing sound of the train whistle and it stung in his nose like air too fresh and too cold. He heard the warm glow and the hot brass of the lamps and the sound seared in his ears. He could hear clearly, succinctly, the sound of a parrot who had never screamed.

Tapping, below it all, ticking as steady as his heart-beat, he heard the thin metal box just under the bed. He waited in the telegraph office at night. It was raining and the tickle of the raindrops at the glass window struck a light rhythm with the straight-key as his finger hovered and dipped, flicking, pausing, translating. The darkness pressed in at the shuttered door and he could feel the force of it straining against the boards of the walls. He could feel the floor shifting subtle beneath his feet. The train was coming into the station.

Underneath all of this, as if this image were the mere thin sheet overlaying a blueprint more complex and more real, he still felt the quilt on the bed and the dense softness of the pillow beneath his head. He saw Charlie watching him, but also moving to the door and opening it and speaking softly but hurriedly to someone just outside the room.

Through both visions, the message came, fast, furious, requiring all of his brain to track and interpret. He did not know how to answer, but he thought perhaps he would not need the straight-key to do so.

.-- .... .- -/.... .- - .... /--. --- -../
.-- .-. --- ..- --. .... -

Author's Note: This story was inspired by the rumors around Edison's interests in the spiritual world, and his quote in the October 1920 issue of *The American Magazine*: "I have been at work for some time building an apparatus to see if it is possible for personalities which have left this earth to communicate with us."

Kings of Glass

Once upon a time past,
if separate times exist,
the sixth Charles of France
let no subjects near
for fear of shattering.
He ordered iron rods
inserted in his clothes
to brace his flasks.
In our murky world,
as far as we perceive,
it would be simpler
surviving as quartz.
Charles in battle
attacked his own men,
destroying his protection.
Less than crystal beings
into shards we smash.

— Linda Neuer

This winter, discover the unexpected with *Tales of the Talisman!*

Hurricane Katrina had a far-reaching impact for New Orleans and the country. Lou Antonelli shows us the impact it had on mermaids.

Frank Tavares shows us that a person really can fly and if they ever get the opportunity, they should relax and enjoy the experience.

Kaiden is a man looking for companionship in a Lovecraftian wasteland. He pleads an elder god for help. As Glynn Owen Barrass asks, what are monsters without someone to scare?

Jude-Marie Green shows us that even starship captains can learn lessons in command through the power of magic.

David B. Riley shows us what happened the year Santa attempted to modernize toy delivery!

These and other thrilling stories await in the winter issue of *Tales of the Talisman!*

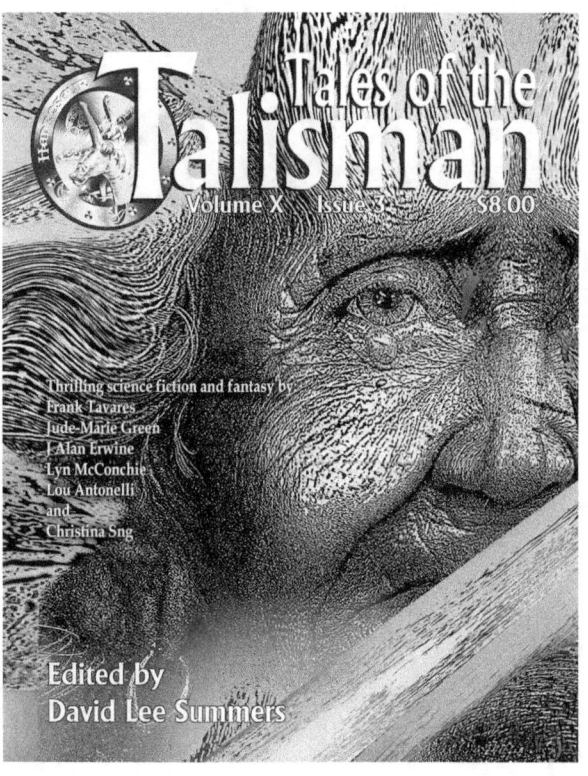

Talisman Book Reviews

Phoenix Island
John Dixon
Gallery Books
19.99, Hardcover
320 Pages

Intelligence
CBS Television
13 Episodes

MEAT: A REVIEW OF *INTELLIGENCE* AND *PHOENIX ISLAND*

John Dixon's novel *Phoenix Island* inspired the CBS show *Intelligence*, but they went their separate ways.

Wasn't that inevitable?

I'll bet they spent more on one day's shooting for *Intelligence* than Dixon spent in ten months on writing his novel. With so much at stake, the big networks can't afford to take risks, to be original. They're the blue chips to Dixon's wild cat speculations.

So *Intelligence* conformed. Take out the brain surgery and it had almost nothing in common with the novel.

Though it was the top new show and star Josh Holloway appeared on the cover of the January 6, 2014 *TV Guide*, by May it was canceled. The changes left something too easily compared to other, more established shows like *Person of Interest* and *Burn Notice*, which also made heroes of ex-Delta Force soldiers and reflected post-9/11 paranoia, conspiracy theories, and delusions of grandeur ("The NSA is reading my emails!") through Hollywood's crackpot-pandering filter.

Dixon's *Phoenix Island*, on the other hand, took a non-conformist JD named Carl Freeman for a hero. He stood up for the little guys and bullied the bullies, so the powers-that-be sent him to a Sparta-like boot camp. Maybe to punish him. Maybe to make him over into something more useful to them.

Dixon was a featured author on the SFWA site. He was also interviewed for *Mystery Scene*. Like Lawrence Block's Tanner series or Donald Westlake's *Smoke*, his *Phoenix Island* straddles genres.

The first twelve chapters blew me away. I liked it best when Dixon was writing what he knows, but that realism and relevance was a point of departure. This thriller then launched into transhuman and dystopic SF tropes about as subtle as a punch in the face.

Dixon's teenaged Freeman became more and more like Captain America, the original super-soldier. The white hat, outnumbered and outgunned, he was trying desperately to save his friends, and you know he's got a fighting chance. After all, he's the Ultimate Human Fighting Machine—if only he'd use brass knuckles or learn to wrestle to keep from breaking the bones in his hands … (America didn't have problems like this.)

And, like a good comic book, the end leaves you hanging. When's that next issue coming out?

January 6, 2015. But you can pre-order *Devil's Pocket* now. In the sequel, "Six months have passed since the events of *Phoenix Island*, and Carl … is sent to a no-holds-barred fighting tournament inside a volcano."

Back in the early 1980s, my step-brother and I acted out that scenario with GI Joe action figures on the sofa cushions. And what kid hasn't played "hot lava" on the playground? That's part of the draw—seeing how Dixon handles this seemingly familiar material. He's a pro. I've been reading his stuff for over decade now. His stories move in the best pulp tradition. He makes likeable characters and he butchers them in interesting ways to show us what they're made of:

Meat that bites back.

— Robert E. Porter

Wendigo
Jeremy Terry
Self-published
$0.99, eBook
110 pages

Wendigo opens on Canada's King William Island. Demonic creatures pursue and surround an Inuit named Tanaruk. With the end clearly near, the scene switches a little further south where a team of researchers gather to join an archeological expedition on the island. This team is led by Dr. Stacy Nelson, a woman who expertly wields throwing knives, but seems to be hiding something from her past. Also on the team are Alaric Downs, a former Army Ranger who is along as a safety officer, David Ujarak, a student originally from King William Island, and Henry Drake, a graduate student. They fly north where they meet Professor R.D.H. Jefferson and his team. The professor proves to be an egotistical jerk who only cares about his research.

As the members of the expedition start their work, they are soon interrupted by a vicious polar bear, then by an Inuit who requests members of the team use their equipment to help search for the missing Tanaruk. Professor Jefferson attempts to blow off the request, but others of the team are more willing to lend a hand. When Stacy, Alaric, and David meet up with the Inuit they learn that Tanaruk had been to a forbidden place. It turns out it's a place where two ships from the nineteenth century attempted to pass, looking for the fabled Northwest Passage. The ships ran aground and the crews died.

The members of the expedition are now motivated not only to attempt to rescue Tanaruk, but recover the lost ships. What they find instead are the demonic creatures Tanaruk already discovered.

Wendigo is a real thrill-ride of a novel. There's not really enough space for a lot of twists and turns or deep character development. However, we get to know the characters well enough that we care about them and the situation is sufficiently engaging that we're pulled along for the ride. Although errors were minimal, a little more rigorous proofreading would have helped. "Alright" is fine for comic books where space is at a premium, but an eBook has the space to expand that to the more formal "all right."

If you like your horror mixed with a little historical intrigue and some serious action, *Wendigo* is a great entertainment deal at 99 cents.

— David Lee Summers

Fallenwood
Leslie D. Soule
Melange Books
$13.95, Trade Paperback
$4.99, Ebook
194 pages

Ashley Kensington, a young woman working a dead-end retail job, has just lost the one person she trusted: her step-father. Overwhelmed during his funeral, she runs away and crosses a portal into the land of Fallenwood, where she soon meets the wizard Will Everett. Will takes Ashley under his wing and shows her that Fallenwood is in danger of being torn apart by the petty squabbles and political machinations of its kingdoms. Feeling a new sense of purpose, Ashley joins Will on a quest to heal the land.

Fallenwood's strength is in its characters. Although plagued by self-doubt and even occasional thoughts of suicide, Ashley's yearning for inner strength appealed to me. I enjoyed spending time with determined Will Everett and his friends, who included the court jester Tercis Solario, the betrayed Prince Edward, and the messenger-turned-cat, Greymalkin. It was even fun to see the wicked Queen Genevieve and the Sorcerer Maskelyne weave their diabolical plots.

Unfortunately, the novel's structure doesn't do the characters justice. Numerous, short chapters bounce back and forth in time, sometimes introducing new characters without context. In some cases, chapter breaks exist simply to shift the point of view character, when a simple scene break would have better retained the narrative flow. Throughout the novel, there are places where I would have liked to have seen how Ashley worked through an emotional problem to push ahead.

Although *Fallenwood* utilizes tropes from other fantasy novels, they're assembled in refreshing ways. It seems the introduction of magic is what ripped Fallenwood from our world, which allows for some shared history. Magic use itself comes with some terrible costs. There's a decidedly vicious unicorn and a set of lovely dragons.

Fallenwood is a short, entertaining, but flawed quest fantasy. That said, I enjoyed spending time with the residents of this new land and I'm pleased to see there are more books in this world.

— David Lee Summers

Much Slower Than Light
Carolyn Clink
Who's That Coeurl? Press
No Price Listed
18 pages

This is the seventh edition of a poetry pamphlet first published in 1996, with additions in subsequent issues. The poems are reprinted from publications such as *Star*Line, On Spec, Space and Time, Transversions, Weird Tales, NoD, Tesseracts* and many others. There are also lists of some of the reprints over the years.

Canadian poet Carolyn Clink begins with "Stars" which "Pinwheel down, down / into a spiral / galaxy, light blueshifting" and "Skylab 1973-1979" with "Fragments of space debris / and me, floating in vacuum / observing the Earth." She ends with "Toronto Necropolis" in which "There are dead men on Yonge / Street. They visit from the / Necropolis near the / park at Riverdale Farm" and an untitled Tanka where "Jade Rabbit / says good night / to planet Earth."

In between you'll find "Halloween in Hell," "Claws & Effect," "If Stephen King Wrote for the Soaps," and of course "Much Slower Than Light." In "Very Large Array" we learn "I am alone here, / if you ignore the herd of cattle grazing / amongst the radio dishes gazing upward." In "The ABCs of the End of the World" we're told "The Amazon burns."

Unfortunately, Clink's poem "Zombie Poet" is

not included. I liked it enough to nominate it for the 2013 Rhysling Award given by the SF Poetry Association. It's worth looking up, just as this pamphlet is worth getting your tentacles on. Highly recommended.

The address for Who's That Coeurl? Press is: PH2-4470 Tucana Court, Mississaugua, Ontario, Canada L5R 3K8.

— Neal Wilgus

About the talisman scale:
Books are ranked on a scale of five talismans with five being the most recommended and one being the least.

Please note: We are no longer accepting books for review. Thanks to all the authors who have kindly provided books for our perusal.

About the Contributors

Christine Marie Angela has been writing stories and poems since she was five years old, though they've gotten a bit more sophisticated over the years. As a child, she was told to get her head out of the clouds and stop writing fairy tales so that she could have a successful life. She has that, now, bur ... she continues to write fairy tales.

M.E. Brines spent the Cold War assembling atomic artillery shells and preparing to unleash the Apocalypse (and has a medal to prove it). But when peace broke out, he turned his fevered, paranoid imagination to other pursuits. He spends his spare time scribbling another steampunk romance occult adventure novel, which despite certain rumors absolutely DOES NOT involve time-traveling Nazi vampires!

A member of the British Society for Psychical Research, he is a long-time student of the occult, a committed Christian, and author of three dozen books, e-books, chapbooks and pamphlets on esoteric subjects such as Alien Abduction, Alien Hybrids, UFOs, Conspiracies, Mind Control the Falun Gong, esoteric Nazism, the Knights Templar, astrology, magick, the Bible, the spear of Longinius and Christian discipleship. His work has also appeared in *Challenge* magazine, *Weird Tales*, *The Traveller Chronicle*, *Midnight Times*, *The Outer Darkness*, *Empirical* and *The Willows* magazine.

Charles Chapman and **David Van Houten** are currently finishing their first novel, *In the Shadow of the Dragon*, an Arthurian fantasy novel. This is their first collaboratively published piece. They live in Huntsville, Texas, where they keep their sanity through their writing.

G.O. Clark's writing has been published in *Asimov's Science Fiction*, *Analog*, *Talebones Magazine*, *Strange Horizons*, *Space & Time*, *RetroSpec: Tales of Fantasy and Nostalgia*, *A Sea of Alone: Poems for Alfred Hitchcock*, *Tales of the Talisman*, *Daily SF*, and many other publications. He's the author of ten poetry collections. The two most recent are: *White Shift*, 2012 Sam's Dot Publishing, and *Scenes Along the Zombie Highway*, 2013 Dark Regions Press. His fiction collection, *The Saucer Under My Bed & Other Stories* was published by Sam's

Dot Publishing in 2011. He won the Asimov's Reader's Award for Poetry in 2001 and has been a repeat Rhysling and Stoker Award nominee. He's retired and lives in Davis, California.

See http://goclarkpoet.weebly.com for more info.

Gary W. Davis has published three gothic poems in *Tales of the Talisman* over the past year. He enjoys writing poetry about classic creatures such as vampires, mummies and werewolves. He recently penned a werewolf transformation poem, entitled "Brain-Sturm." Mr. Davis also loves all things Halloween. In 2014, he wrote a short ghost story, "She Didn't Forget Halloween," and an essay, "Zen Philosophy for Halloween," which takes an Eastern holistic approach to some of the strange and diverse practices of Western Halloween culture.

T. Fox Dunham resides outside of Philadelphia PA—author and historian. He's published in nearly 200 international journals and anthologies. His first novel, *The Street Martyr* was published by Gutter Books this October, followed by *Professional Detachment*, a literary erotica from Bitten Press and followed by *Searching for Andy Kaufman* from PMMP in 2014. He's a cancer survivor. His friends call him fox, being his totem animal, and his motto is: Wrecking civilization one story at a time.

Site: www.tfoxdunham.com.
Blog: http://tfoxdunham.blogspot.com.
Facebook: http://www.facebook.com/tfoxdunham
Twitter: @TFoxDunham

A frequent contributor to both *Tales of the Talisman* and *Hadrosaur Tales*, **Gary Every** is the author of the science fiction novella *The Saint and the Robot*, which is based upon a medieval legend concerning the youth of Thomas Aquinas. *Shadow of the OhshaD*, a collection of the best of his award winning newspaper columns about Arizona's Native Americans, history, and environment is also available at Amazon.com or his website www.garyevery.com

As a child, **Kathy Ferrell** refused to share her crayons, preferring to eat them all herself. Today she is an artist and writer working from her decidedly sinister 19th century home, nestled deep in the backwoods of Appalachia. When not creating, she can be found wrapped in a shawl, drinking tea and wondering what on earth could be making that incessant creaking on the stair. She also uses the internet, in spite of being warned.

Paintings: cuposwank.carbonmade.com
Words: cuposwank.wordpress.com

Neil T. Foster is a freelance artist who lives in Australia. He has penciled and inked various comic books, recently completing an online comic—*Beware the Beast*—for the official International *Planet of the Apes* Fan Club. He has done illustrations and painted covers for various SF fanzines, CD booklets and computer games. His work includes everything from illustration, cartoons, logos and comic strips to artwork for action figure packaging. His illustrations and painting have also appeared in *The Corpse* and *Black Petals* Magazines.

Karin L. Frank's poems have been published or are forthcoming in *Asimov's, Dark Matter Journal, Dreams and Nightmares* and in previous issues of *Tales of the Talisman*. In April 2012, her first book of poems entitled *A Meeting of Minds* was released. Except for the illustrations, it is entirely a work of speculative poetry.

Raymond H.V. Gallucci is a Professional Engineer who has been writing poetry since 1990. He is an incorrigible rhymer, tending toward the skeptical/cynical regarding daily life. He has been fortunate to have been published in poetry magazines and on-line journals such as *Nuthouse, Mother Earth International, Feelings/Poets' Paper, Möbius, Pablo Lennis, Muse of Fire, So Young!, The Aardvark Adventurer, Poetic License, Thumbprints, Unlikely Stories, Bibliophilos, Fullosia Press, Nomad's Choir, Hidden Oak, Poetsespresso, Soul Fountain, Writers' Journal, Atlantic Pacific Press, Ceremony/The Sheltered Poet, Deronda Review, Lyric, The Storyteller, Write On!, Tales of the Talisman* and *Dana Literary Society*.

R. Donald James Gauvreau maintains a blog at www.whitemarbleblock.blogspot.com, where he regularly posts story ideas, free fiction, and other goodies, including a free guide to comparative mythology that was written specifically with worldbuilding in mind. He writes columns for *Sanitarium* Magazine, RPG.net, and *Seventh Sanctum*, among others.

Laura Givens is a Denver Based author and artist. Her art has graced the covers of numerous publishers' books and magazines. She has provided illustrations for *Orson Scott Card's Intergalactic Medicine Show, Jim Baen's Universe, Talebones, Science Fiction Trails* and *Tales of the Talisman*. Her work may be viewed at www.lauragivens-artist.com. In 2010 she naively decided she could probably write stories as good as many she had illustrated. She has sold works ranging from zombie stories to space operas. She was co-editor and contributor to *Six-Guns Straight From Hell*, a weird western anthology, and is art director for *Tales of the Talisman* magazine.

Morland Gonsoulin is a traditionally trained artist and avid science fiction fan living in Colorado Springs, Colorado. He has done artwork for various publications before, including *Tales of the Talisman* Magazine.

K.S. Hardy has had fantasy poetry appear in many publications over the years including *Dreams and Nightmares, Not One of Us, Mythic Delirium*, and more. Short stories of a like nature have been featured in *Tales of the Talisman, Beyond Centauri*, and *Lore* (drawing comment from Brian Lumly). He has been nominated for a Rhysling Award. And his first children's book *Her Best Trick or Treat, Ever* with a safe, scary theme has just come out. Signed copies are exclusively available through Library House Children's Books, Grand Rapids, Ohio 43522.

C.J. Killmer was born and raised in the Sunshine State, where he misspent his childhood swimming with sharks and alligators, searching the Everglades for the elusive Skunk Ape (Florida's Sasquatch) and in general avoiding any danger of becoming a respectable member of society. He currently spends his days teaching college history, but when the sun goes down, he writes horror, sci-fi, and crime stories. His stories have appeared in *Science Fiction Trails, Tales of the Talisman, Ray Gun Revival*, and a variety of anthologies, including *Dead Bait, Low Noon*, and *Gunslingers & Ghost Stories*.

Jag Lall works in both the comic book industry and book illustration field producing bold, atmospheric artwork. The former is his lifeblood and he is currently working on a project to raise awareness of different cultures.

Lyn Lifshin has published more than 130 books and chapbooks and edited four anthologies of women writers. Her work has appeared in most literary and poetry magazines. She has been included in virtually every major anthology. She has given more than 700 readings across the U.S.A. and has been Poet in Residence at Rochester, Antioch and Colorado Mountain College. Winner of the Jack Kerouac Award for her book *Kiss the Skin Off*, Lyn is the subject of the documentary film, just released, *Lyn Lifshin: Not Made of Glass*.

Lifshin's recent books include *All the Poets Who Touched Me, Living and Dead: All True, Especially the Lies* and *For the Roses*, poems for Joni Mitchell and *Knife Edge & Absinthe: The Tango Poems, Hotel Hitchcock* and just out Fall of 2013: *Tangled as the Alphabet: The Istanbul Poems* and *A Girl Goes Into the Woods*. *Malala* was just published.

Forthcoming books include: *Secretariat: The Red Freak, The Miracle, Luminous Women: Eneduanna, Scheherazade, Nefertiti*. Also forthcoming: the 2002-2013 update to Gale Research autobiography series: *Lips, Blues, Blue Lace: On the Outside*. Her website for more books, photos, prose, and news is www.lynlifshin.com

Dan Manning lives and writes in Grand Rapids, MI. He is the author of *Android Down, Firewood for Cannibals (and other stories), The Cubicles of Madness, Get Your Zen On* and *Zen Happens*.

His books can be found at his website: www.danmanning.com.

Faith, nature, molecular biology (a former researcher) and membership in the SFPA help to inspire **Lauren McBride's** stories and poems, which have appeared in various science fiction, fantasy, horror, nature and children's publications including *Dreams and Nightmares, The Magazine of Speculative Poetry* and *Star*Line*. She shares a love of laughter, science and the ocean with her husband and two children.

Linda Neuer is from Miami, Florida. Recently, some of her poems have been published in *Jupiter, Quantum Poetry Magazine, Tattoo Highway, Lily, Sangam, Abyss and Apex*, and *Astropoetica*. Also she have had a chapbook published.

Paul Niemiec plays guitar in a swing band—atomic pablo. Check it out at myspace.com. Paul's first job in high school was an art job doing safety filmstrips for hard-rock miners. After that, the office situation—smooth jazz radio, and chain-smoking co-workers—really put him off commercial art.

After a long hiatus, he got back into drawing. Paul was trying to figure out which way a camel's front legs bent, and he decided to go to the zoo to draw camels. Later, he met some of the Squid Works guys at a figure drawing class.

Richard P. Nixon is an avid science fiction fan who writes and lives in Mesa, Arizona. He grew up in boarding school mostly in Northern Ireland during The Troubles, living in Saudi Arabia, and traveling around the world. He missed out on the original *Star Wars* fun, but gained a well-rounded appreciation of different cultures, both the good and the bad, which he draws upon in his upcoming sci-fi novel *The Peace Makers*.

Rick Novy lives in Scottsdale, Arizona. His education is technical, holding degrees in physics, mathematics, and engineering. Through his career, he has flown satellites, helped develop surgical implants, and worked with various integrated circuits and sensors. He is now a freelance writer and also teaches in the mathematics department at the local community college.

Rick started writing seriously in the summer of 2004. In 2005, he attended Orson Scott Card's Literary Boot Camp. Since that workshop, his fiction has appeared dozens of times in both online and print venues. His novels, *Neanderthal Swan Song, Rigel Kentaurus*, and *Fishpunk* are available at most major online retailers everywhere.

Learn more: www.ricknovy.com

Aaron Polson currently lives in Lawrence, Kansas with his wife and six children. He's now at full sitcom. To pay the bills, he counsels high school students about post-graduation plans, but he's still not sure what he wants to be when he grows up. His short fiction has appeared *in Shock Totem, Shimmer, Bourbon Penn*, and under several unsavory rocks. Rumor has it he prefers ketchup with his beans.

Robert E. Porter has gone to ground somewhere in the Midwest with his cat, his laptop, and a library card. His nonfiction credits include "Some Hope For Us All" forthcoming in *Scifaikuest*.

LB Sedlacek's poems have been published in publications such as *The Speculative Edge, Mastodon Dentist,*

RiverLit, Main Street Rag, The Copperfield Review, Third Wednesday, Fickle Muses, Apparent Magnitude, Sea Stories, and others.

Abra Staffin-Wiebe spent several years living abroad in India and Africa before marrying a mad scientist and settling down to live and write in Minneapolis. She specializes in dark science fiction, cheerful horror, and modern fairy tales. She also maintains Aswiebe's Market List, a resource for science fiction, fantasy, and horror writers. Discover more of her fiction at her website, http://www.aswiebe.com, or find her on the social media site of your choice.

Jason Sturner grew up along the Fox River in northern Illinois. Of his many jobs, those he most enjoyed were naturalist and botanist. His stories and poems have appeared in *Space and Time Magazine, Star*Line, Tales of the Talisman, Morpheus Tales,* and *Liquid Imagination,* among others. He currently lives in Knoxville, Tennessee, near the Great Smoky Mountains. Website: www.jasonsturner.blogsopot.com.

Erin K. Wagner is an avid writer and, more importantly, reader of sci-fi and fantasy. She is also a doctoral candidate in Medieval English literature and is in the midst of a dissertation that may be her most intimidating writing project to date. However, composing short stories and a novel-in-progress allow her to relax and imagine a world not quite so grounded in historical fact. This is her first short story publication. Her poetry has appeared in the *South Dakota Review.*

Neal Wilgus is a throwback to the Typewriter Age so you won't find him online. Despite being ignored or banned by some internet publications, Neal manages to publish over 60 poems each year in the US and UK, much of it is SF/F/H. His poems have been nominated for the Rhysling Award (US) and the Data Dump Award (UK) several times. He also does a short story or two each year, two of which have won the fiction competition at the *Oasis Journal* annual anthology. He is s a regular reviewer for Small Press Review and contributes long narrative poems to the New York monthly tabloid *The Sovereign.* His study of conspiracy theories, *The Illuminoids* (1978), is still in print, as are several chapbooks of poetry and a collection of his *Leak News Service* satires. He still uses carbon paper.

Mike Wilson has been writing short fiction and poetry for a decade. He has three collections of short stories out, and is working on a fourth. All of his stories are available on amazon.com.

Vaughn Wright is a long-term prisoner and Philly native whose work has most recently appeared in *J Journal, Thema, PKA's Advocate,* and *Pearl.* This is his third time appearing in *Talisman,* which he considers an enormous honor.

A collection of his short stories, *Tales from the Inside,* can be viewed at www.PrisonsFoundation.org.

Lee Clark Zumpe has been writing and publishing horror, dark fantasy and speculative fiction since the late 1990s. His short stories and poetry have appeared in a variety of publications such as *Weird Tales, Space and Time* and *Dark Wisdom;* and in anthologies such as *Horrors Beyond, Corpse Blossoms, Best New Zombie Tales Vol. 3, Cthulhu Unbound Vol. 1* and *Future Lovecraft.* His work has earned several honorable mentions in *The Year's Best Fantasy and Horror* collections.

An entertainment columnist with Tampa Bay Newspapers, Lee has penned hundreds of film, theater and book reviews and has interviewed novelists as well as music industry icons such as Paddy Moloney of The Chieftains and Alan Parsons. His work for TBN has been recognized repeatedly by the Florida Press Association, including a first place award for criticism in the 2007 Better Weekly Newspaper Contest.

Lee lives on the west coast of Florida with his wife and daughter. Visit www.leeclarkzumpe.com.